HAPPY ENDINGS

Tina Devino is a moderately successful author, who aspires to bestsellerdom. As do her clients, because Tina is also a 'literary consultant', who uses her own experience to advise other would-be authors. But Tina's own life leaves a lot to be desired – her lover is drifting away, and her position on the Salubrious fiction list is threatened by more glamorous writers. Can Tina achieve the fame, fortune and happy ending to which she aspires?

Trisha Ashley titles available from
Severn House Large Print

Sweet Nothings
The Generous Gardener

HAPPY ENDINGS

Trisha Ashley

Severn House Large Print
London & New York

This first large print edition published 2010
in Great Britain and the USA by
SEVERN HOUSE PUBLISHERS LTD of
9-15 High Street, Sutton, Surrey, SM1 1DF.
First world regular print edition published 2008 by
Severn House Publishers Ltd., London and New York.

British Library Cataloguing in Publication Data

Ashley, Trisha.
  Happy endings.
  1. Women novelists, English--Fiction. 2. Love stories.
  3. Large type books.
  I. Title
  823.9'2-dc22

  ISBN-13: 978-0-7278-7865-6

Severn House Publishers support The Forest Stewardship
Council [FSC], the leading international forest certification
organisation. All our titles that are printed on Greenpeace-
approved FSC-certified paper carry the FSC logo.

Mixed Sources
Product group from well-managed
forests and other controlled sources
www.fsc.org Cert no. SA-COC-1565
© 1996 Forest Stewardship Council

Printed and bound in Great Britain by the
MPG Books Group, Bodmin, Cornwall.

For Katie Fforde – a constant inspiration

Acknowledgements

I'd like to thank my agent, Judith Murdoch, for all her endeavours on my behalf over the years, though I am happy to say that, despite occasionally performing miracles, she bears no other resemblance to the Miracle of the book.

One

In a Jiffy

Because you are my sister,
I'll take the time to say,
I wish you health and happiness,
On this, your *special day.*

Because you are my sister,
Though our ways have grown apart,
I'll always take you with me,
Right here, in my heart.

For Tina,
With love from Antonio and all the bambinos

So it's my birthday, and I'm not saying which one because it's so *middle-aged* I can't believe it's true, and someone *has* to be playing a bad joke on me. My friend Linny gave me one of those little Dictaphone things because she said I had an interesting life and should record my great thoughts right off the top of my head, just in the terribly spontaneous way I always spoke.

'And look how those American universities

9

snap up an author's entire collection of scrap paper, so what *wouldn't* they give in a few years' time when you are rich and famous for actual *recordings* of the great Tina Devino's voice?'

I said that by the time I was rich and famous, technology would probably have made anything other than interactive holograms obsolete and then she said I watched too many ancient *Star Trek* reruns.

However, I'm happy to admit that I am an absolute sucker for people with knobbly faces wearing giant stretch Babygros and so cannot get enough of that type of programme.

'*You* can't talk, Linny, because anyone who watches old Buffy episodes shouting, "Bite me! Bite me!" whenever Spike appears is a truly sad person,' I pointed out, and she went all defensive.

But anyway, Linny hasn't been gone five minutes and this is my first recording, so I can see I'm going to be absolutely *addicted* to talking to myself, because *naturally* I'm my biggest fan; and whenever two writers are gathered together, let's face it, it's not so much a question of conversation but more a case of, 'Let's talk about something more interesting, darling: me, me, *me!*'

Linny had arrived wearing a black T-shirt

with B.B.B.B. on the back, and the words Big, Buxom, Brunette and Beautiful emblazoned across her chest in sequins, but that still left plenty of room; she could have added Batty and Bossy as well. I bet that caused a stir when she walked through Shrimphaven on the way to my humble little fisherman's cottage (unfortunately *sans* fisherman). She doesn't often deign to visit me as she lives in Primrose Hill, which is much more interesting to someone like me who desires to live the Literary Life to the full. So I visit her instead, especially when Tertius the Tycoon is away, which is a lot of the time. And also my lover Sergei, the ex-ballet dancer turned exercise guru, lives nearby.

You *must* have heard of Sergei Popov? Even if you aren't into ballet (I'm not) or exercise (ditto – or not out of bed, anyway), I bet you have his SergeiYoga DVD, just for the pleasure of watching him bending his beautifully supple body into strange positions while looking dead sexy.

It is lucky that the train service between Shrimphaven and London is fast and frequent, for I spend huge amounts of time shuttling up and down between the two. But, like Trollope, I find travelling terribly conducive to creative thought and so write much of my novels on the way, penned into large notebooks hand-bound by my friend Jackie (when she isn't making enormous quantities of totally useless paper flowers).

Linny had brought one of the sequinned T-shirts for me, but I said, 'Linny, you should have had the "Big" deleted from mine because, let's face it, I'm vertically challenged so my bust measurement is almost the same as my height.'

'Yes,' she said, 'but it could be Big as in Bestseller – you're going to be *huge*! I can feel it in my waters.'

Yuk.

Then she ate the big box of Godiva chocolates Sergei sent me, so she's the one who is going to tip over the scales into huge at any moment.

Next morning found me printing off a new batch of flyers:

NOVELTINA LITERARY AND CRITICAL AGENCY MANUSCRIPT ASSESSMENT SERVICE

Dear aspiring novelist,
By contacting Noveltina you have taken the first step on the long and rocky road to success as a writer. If you send me your manuscript you can expect to receive a full and constructive criticism that, if fol-

lowed, will increase its chance of acceptance by a publisher. Yes, I am that vital stepping stone between the beginning novelist and the published!

I hope that we can work together to achieve your dreams, and I look forward to receiving your manuscript, double-spaced and in clear type, in the near future, plus a cheque made out to T. Devino for the sum of three hundred pounds, which covers manuscripts up to one hundred and fifty thousand words.

Yours sincerely,
Tina Devino

Like it? It's my little money-making side-line, and so much more fun than the secretarial temping that I was never very good at anyway, being a fast but totally inaccurate typist easily distracted by thoughts of new plot twists. I suppose it was amazing that I had *any* original ideas while temping, though, because all the offices seemed to have been hermetically sealed full of sterile dust at birth and therefore incapable of nurturing anything but recycled thoughts – and if there *is* any nutritive jelly in the Petri dish of the business world, I didn't find it.

I only place one advertisement a year in the *Writers' & Artists' Yearbook*, yet get a steady stream of manuscripts of all kinds, and not only am I good at it but I can fit it around the rest of my life and my own writing, so it's a terribly convenient way of surviving until I have my bestseller.

When the postman rang I tossed the flyers aside and sprang like a hungry tigress for the door because he never rings twice. His finger barely touches the doorbell button before he is sneaking off down the path again and I have to leap out regardless of how I am dressed (or undressed) to drag him back into my lair. After that he spends half an hour slowly fingering the post in his bag before reluctantly handing over whatever it is that's mine.

This time you'd think he would have been glad to get rid of the weight, because someone has sent me the most *enormous* manuscript for a critique, and I didn't know Jiffy bags came in gigantic, although the cheque certainly didn't, because I can see with a glance that there is a lot more than the one hundred and fifty thousand words he's paid me for! Besides that, I was *deeply* disappointed that it wasn't a late birthday present, although this sort of thing *is* my bread and butter, so really I should fall on anything that helps me to pay the mortgage on my picturesque heap of loosely connected beach pebbles with loud cries of joy.

Just listen to this:

The Ramblings,
Bosson Surcoat,
Cresney

Dear Ms Devino,
    I enclose a synopsis and manuscript of my thriller, Banking On It, *together with the cheque you requested and a stamped addressed envelope.*
    I will be pleased to have your critique of the work as soon as possible, for although all my friends and family assure me that it is a fast, pacy and exciting book that they would beg to buy in the shops, the reactions of the publishers and agents to whom I have submitted it have not so far been encouraging – in fact, in some cases it does not appear that the manuscript has actually been read – so perhaps I am simply presenting the work in the wrong way?
    It is topical and set in the thrilling world of international accounting, which I am well qualified to describe, but it also has ecological implications that give it an extra dimension, and I know you will be swept away by the scale of the epic story as it unfolds. Several of my friends have said that they are so amazed by the breadth of it that they simply don't know how to describe it.
    I expect you have male readers working for your agency, who will be more suited to assessing a work of this type, since it is definitely a man's novel.
    I look forward to your prompt response.
    Yours sincerely,
    Harold Snaith, ACA

Doesn't exactly sound a laugh-a-minute, does it? I read the letter out to Sergei when he phoned later to tell me about some minor ailment that was troubling him (he's such a hypochondriac!), and he was quite indignant.

'Why must you do this work – this *drudgery*?' he demanded, as though I'd been gulagged into the salt mines. 'You have a soul above these things, my darling.'

'I don't have a soul above paying the mortgage, though,' I pointed out. 'And actually, I'm good at it. It will be ironic if I help someone become a bestseller while I'm still languishing in the mid-list, won't it?'

'To me, you are always a star,' he said simply. 'Tsarina Tina!'

You have to love a man with a beguiling accent who makes bad jokes.

Monday morning came around, and I was sitting in Sergei's basement flat wondering how our red-hot passion had dwindled down to a once-a-week habit followed by Russian tea from his samovar and accompanied by caviar – and though I totally hate those glistening little fish eggs I expect the iodine is good for me and I'll never get a goitre – but it might make you *wonder* because he's definitely a bit Nureyev. Mind you, he may

16

only be teaching SergeiYoga and the odd ballet masterclass now, rather than performing, but he can still jump with the best of them, so I'd be deeply unwilling to think the worst of him even if he does wear eyeliner in bed and is as vain as a budgie: give him a mirror and he's happy for *hours*. Besides, he's never given me cause to suspect he's anything other than one hundred per cent heterosexual male.

But how did we get to this stage? And what is he doing the rest of the week, other than overseeing SergeiYoga classes at his studio in Primrose Square, going to the ballet, and hanging out with his dancing chums and various dubious-looking arty Russian émigrés until all hours? Maybe it's better not to know.

Of course, when we are apart he still phones me at least once a day, with a bulletin about his imaginary ailments and all his little troubles, but he has been distracted lately. Well, I say *lately*, but it's been about a year actually, and it does make me speculate about whether there's someone else in his life – or even *several* someones? I'm sure Linny would love to be one of them, despite having a perfectly good husband of her own and finding Sergei a little scary, even though I told her that although he has a beautiful body, his feet look like loose bundles of old rope knotted around twigs.

When we *do* go out together he is always being recognized, because not only is he famed for his years of leading roles with the Royal Ballet, not to mention the SergeiYoga DVD and accompanying book, but he also has an exotic face and a magnetic personality, which is good for my Brilliant Career too, because I do try and plug my books whenever I get a chance; and quite frankly I'm tired of being a hanger-on at the fringes of London literary life. I want a piece of the action.

But now I only generally see him on Monday mornings and the furthest we ever get is to walk round to the Lemonia for lunch occasionally. He just seems to want to stay at home, though perhaps he's simply getting older. And so am I (older than he thinks!) and sometimes now when he leaps on me I'm not sure I've got the stamina any more and I wish someone would ring a bell and end the bout.

Mind you, I have always been aware that he has this other life, because I could have become part of it when we first embarked on our grand passion. But I chose not to because despite loving him madly I simply couldn't do with all that *ballet*, not to mention all the arty types draped around his flat most evenings, any more than I could do

18

with my ex-husband's mania for football. I am not prepared to fake enthusiasm for *anything*, including bad sex (fortunately *not* a consideration with Sergei), besides not liking to live with anyone, so clearly I am not cut out for marriage or indeed any other kind of permanent relationship. Sergei says I remind him of his beloved cat Petruschka (deceased), which is good, but Linny says I have the emotional depth of a small puddle and when I have finally lost my looks I will decline into a lonely and embittered spinster.

Anyway, that Monday morning after tea and fish eggs I staggered round to Linny's to recover before I caught the train home. It's quite a walk really because although Sergei always *says* he lives in Primrose Hill, his garden flat is actually on the furthest fringes of Chalk Farm and you'd drop off it if you went further, while Linny is in the posh part and can see famous geriatric dads playing outside with their second or third marriage toddlers any day of the week.

Poor Linny was in absolute despair because the publishers weren't taking on any new writers unless they were skinny blonde twenty-somethings with interesting connections, and look at *her*, fat, dark and the wrong side of forty, with a facial hair problem. I wouldn't say she looks like a walrus because she's one of my best friends, but she should get that 'tache waxed more often and – where was I? Oh, yes, so we had coffee and I agreed it was all dreadful, and it was so hard to break in with a first novel, and yes, rejection was really hard to take – so personal, when your novels are just like your *babies*, and what on earth could she do?

So then I suggested she stopped stuffing her novels into filing cabinet drawers and actually sent them out to editors or agents. (Or even me!) She burst into tears and said she couldn't possibly *show* anybody one of her efforts, could she? And I said I couldn't think of any other way of getting published and she told me I was a *hard* woman.

When I got home I was exhausted as usual, although I had had a refreshing glimpse of Tube Man in London, the dark, stubbly chinned, handsome hunk who has fuelled my fantasies for some time now, and inspired the hero of my last three novels and my new one, even though I fear he might only be a figment of my fevered imagination.

Sometimes I dream that I'm struggling through a crowded tube carriage towards him, and then all the arms barring the way turn into thorny branches that hold me fast while he smiles sadly and turns away ... and why do I *never* dream I've got a pair of secateurs in my hand?

So, with one thing and another, I wasn't quite in the mood when this woman phoned me at eight and said, 'Hello? Is that Tina Devino?'

'It was the last time I looked in the mirror,' I admitted cautiously.

'Well, I...' There was a short pause, followed by a harrumphing noise that wouldn't have disgraced a meditative bison. 'I,' she announced grandly, in the kind of voice usually heard through a megaphone at horse shows, 'I am the president of the local branch of the WFIA—'

'The *what*?'

'Women For Intellectual Advancement, Ms Devino. I discovered from the library that you are a local author, and although you only write *romance*, I thought my little group might get something out of a talk by you.'

I am quite accustomed to these insults, so I said that was kind of her, but I didn't do many talks because I was a bit busy trying to earn a living, and how much were they thinking of paying me?

'Oh, we don't pay our speakers! It is very prestigious to be asked to address us at all – quite an honour – and who knows where it might lead?'

'If I spent all my time talking for nothing it would lead to bankruptcy,' I informed her shortly. 'I mean, you don't call a plumber out and expect them to work for nothing, do you?'

'That is *hardly* the same thing,' she snapped. 'Ramona Gullet, the famous crime novelist, recently gave us some fascinating insights into criminal psychology and *she* certainly didn't ask for any fee, despite being terribly well known and respected!'

The inference being, of course, that I was not.

'Bully for her!' I said.

The woman turned all frosty and said she was sorry she'd ever asked me because I was clearly not quite what they were looking for, and then she put the phone down.

Two

Fluffed

NOVELTINA LITERARY AND
CRITICAL AGENCY
Mudlark Cottage, The Harbour, Shrimphaven.

Dear Miss Noritake,
Thank you for your recent letter.
No, of course I wasn't insinuating that your first language isn't English! I advise all my writers to ask a friend with a particularly good grasp of English to read through their manuscript and indicate any words where the meaning is not quite apposite to the situation.
Also, I did point out that although readers would love your colourful description of the pretty seaside village of Luton, especially the annual Dragon Dance along the sea wall, they might also be confused by the fact that there actually is a city called Luton, which is about as land-locked as it is possible to get. Nor is it much noted for its cherry blossom.

These are all minor criticisms of your slight but poetic work, and I would urge you to make the changes I suggest before submitting it to the Arts Council for one of their grants as you intend – for I think, with a few minor tweaks, it will be just the sort of literary novel they are looking for and you stand every chance of some funding to continue your inspired and deeply meaningful work.

Yours sincerely,
Tina Devino

Jackie – one of my oldest and dearest Shrimphaven friends – just caught me nattering away and she said, 'Tina, why are you talking to yourself?'

And I said, 'I'm not, I'm talking into this dictating machine that Linny gave me for my birthday. It's got teeny tiny cassette tapes in it, and I've had to buy a teeny tiny cassette tape player to go with it.'

Then she cut to the chase and said, 'You had a *birthday*? Which one?'

And I told her I didn't *really* have birthdays any more, because if you don't have them you won't get any older, will you?

'Michael Jackson seems to have the same idea, only I hope you won't resort to surgery,' she said worriedly.

'Probably not, unless I get those deep channels round my mouth like a river estuary, and even then only as a last resort,'

I assured her.

But she was right about me talking to myself, because I was, and it's getting to be a compulsive habit, so who knows? I might end up dictating my books from a chaise longue like Barbara Cartland, but *without* all the pink and *with* all the sex. I'm sure I read somewhere that she left instructions that the leaves from the tree she was buried under were to be given to writer types, but I don't know why, unless it's for inspiration. Anyway, if I get a dead leaf in the post at least I will have some idea what it is, though what can you do with one leaf? I suppose it would make a bookmark, but it would probably *swoon* if pressed between the pages of some of *my* novels.

Jackie had come to ask me to one of her parties the following Friday, and I said I would, because you can't get out of it when it's one of your friends, can you? Though really I like to keep Party Animal Tina and Shrimphaven Seaside Casual Tina quite separate, and sometimes I think Sergei would have a fit if he saw me on the shingle with my hair blown into knots and a mack and wellies ... or maybe not. You never quite know with Sergei, but goings-on on the beach would get me drummed out of the place, that's for sure – if I didn't get pneumonia first, that is. I'm not convinced that would be quite the right kind of publicity, tempting though it is, and, anyway, I'm fond of my little cottage.

Linny went quiet for three days, which was almost unheard of, and then she phoned me and said I was quite right about sending her manuscripts out, and she'd just posted three of them to different publishers and now she couldn't sit still, wondering when she would hear.

'I wouldn't hold your breath – without an agent it might be months.'

'Do you think Miracle would take me on?' she asked hopefully. Miracle Threaple being my agent.

'Not unless you can transform yourself into the beautiful, born-again blonde, twenty-something daughter of a famous family – or a journalist with connections.'

'Well, she took *you* on, Tina, and you're none of those things!'

'Yes, I am, I'm beautiful!' I said indignantly, and of course I'm also brilliant, but modesty prevented me from adding that.

'My great-aunt Vava in Beirut was a famous beauty.'

'No, Linny, she was *notorious*, that's different,' I said. 'You're scraping the bottom of the barrel, though I'm not saying raking up a few old skeletons wouldn't be good for publicity when you do get published, because I got loads of mileage out of being left a lonely orphan at an early age, and banished off to boarding school.'

My poor brother Tony, who is fifteen years my elder (I was a surprise latecomer) and at the time unmarried, simply didn't know what else to do with me. In any case, he was fully occupied running the family business.

'Once you got to school, you weren't lonely – you had me,' she pointed out, which was quite true, but wouldn't have made half as good publicity and anyway, I *was* lonely before we met.

Palazzo Devino,
Nr Cowbridge,
South Wales

Dear Tina,

Christmas is nearly here, and as Maria points out to me, blood is thicker than water, and you are my only sister and so we will expect you to spend the Christmas season with us as usual. All the bambinos, even little Fabia, ask often after their Auntie Tina, though I would be grateful if you choose their Christmas presents with a little more thought than you give to their birthday presents, which Maria and I frequently find unsuitable, especially that magazine subscription you gave Bruno for his sixteenth birthday.

Let me know which train you are getting so I can meet you,
Your affectionate brother,
Antonio

Dear Tony,
From the tone (joke!) of your letter I infer that you have been reading The Godfather again. I do wish you wouldn't.

But thank you for your invitation to spend Christmas with you, Mary and the children as usual, which I will accept providing you don't go on and on about my living in sin and committing adultery like last year, which certainly cast a blight on the festivities; and besides, I don't live with anyone, I'm not married, and even if I did it is none of your business.

I'm afraid I will only be able to spend two nights with you, though, due to pressure of work, and I will drive myself down, because I haven't forgotten how you collected me from the station in a vintage Devino Curly Cone ice-cream van last year, which is pure affectation when you have a perfectly good Mercedes in the driveway – and family roots might lie in ice cream but their lifeblood these days is coffee. At the rate you are expanding, every town in South Wales will soon have at least one Café Devino.

Your affectionate sister,
Tina

I do hate private parties, don't you? There's always someone who gets you in a corner and tells you at enormous length about the wonderful novel they've written, and how it's all *absolutely* from their own life experience, only it's got a *truly* original plot, and if they sent it to an agent or an editor someone might *steal* it, mightn't they? Which, sure enough, is what happened last night at Jackie's party. I told this woman that no, they wouldn't steal her marvellous idea even if she'd got one, but I didn't say that she looked like she'd never had an original thought in her life, because she was bigger than me – though that's not difficult, practically everyone over the age of twelve is bigger than me as I'm only five feet two inches tall.

So *then* she said she'd allow me to read it as a great favour and I said thanks very much but I was much too busy writing my own to read other people's except for money. She said I'd soon feel differently once I'd read *Clacton Stole My Heart* and she'd drop it off the next day and then she just went.

If I find out who gave her my address they are *straight* off my Christmas card list because, lo and behold, there was a cardboard box on my porch this morning when I staggered down, with a note saying here was her baby and to be gentle with it. It wasn't a small box either. And when I opened the lid there wasn't a manuscript in there at all, just a stiff moggy, so I rang the number on the letter and she went hysterical and said she must have buried the manuscript instead of poor Fluffy, who passed away while she was at the party, and did I think that was a bad omen?

I said no, I thought it was just carelessness and what did she want me to do with Fluffy?

She said she'd have to go out and dig up her manuscript like that Pre-Raphaelite poet did, you know, the one who put all his poems in his lover's coffin and then had a change of heart later and had her dug up? Only Fluffy wasn't in there with it, fortunately. And then she said she'd be round later to swap boxes and I said I could hardly wait, and she'd find Fluffy in the porch.

Sergei took me to the Lemonia for lunch on Monday, which I felt I had quite deserved after a morning spent being Spring, scattering daisies in the path of the rampant faun or something – I never seem to quite grasp his plots – and Russian tea and fish eggs would simply not have been sustaining enough to get me home.

But actually we were celebrating my new book, *Spring Breezes*, which had quietly sneaked out wearing its hardback just before

Christmas as usual. Salubrious Press saves what little publicity budget they award me for the paperback in the new year.

At lunchtime, the Lemonia tends to be full of youngish actors, pop stars, models and other minor celebs (and occasionally one or two major celebs) and you can tell immediately which are the waiters and which are famous because the waiters are all better dressed, taller, and more handsome.

Everyone recognized Sergei, which is not surprising, what with enough personal magnetism to cure anyone rheumatic within twenty paces, not to mention the huge wolfskin collar pulled up around his pointy little ears, though thank goodness it is so flamboyant it looks fake, so no one actually ever gets on to the exploitation of animals. The poor thing has been dead for *centuries* anyway because an ancestor in Russia actually shot it when it was chasing him ... and where was I?

Oh, yes – so I was glad I was wearing something trendy without being mutton dressed as lamb, though I only discovered when I got home later (after the usual tube and train journey) that I still had two daisies (silk, but very realistic) tangled in my hair, and when I phoned Sergei to demand why he hadn't told me, he simply said: 'But they suited you, Tsarina!' (Tsarina is the silly pet name he calls me by, though considering what happened to the last one, he could have chosen something more auspicious.) So I couldn't really say any more, could I? Hopefully it will be put down to eccentricity, which is allowable in an author.

When we came out of the Lemonia, a photographer took our picture – Sergei just automatically falls into photogenic poses all the time – and when he was asked for the name of his companion he said very grandly that I was his dear friend Tina Devino, author of many, many famous novels, and he was surprised they didn't know that. I must say that he has always seemed proud of me whenever we are out in public, it's just a pity we don't get out more often, but these days I'm sure my body couldn't stand seeing Sergei more than once a week, if that, and sometimes I'm just happy to settle for the tea and fishy nibbles.

My picture was in one of the tabloids, and I didn't look bad if I say it myself, except for the slight rabbit-caught-in-the-headlights impression, with my eyes stretched wide open and a slightly drunken daisy over one ear.

Tertius took Linny there for dinner the next night and she said her Rich Bitch friends were all talking about how cutting-edge-of-fashion I'd looked, with my slightly prom-style dress and the flowers, and did I think that sort of thing would suit her? So I said she was built on more statuesque lines than me and so should go for a classical Greek draped look instead, and was she all right, because she looked *very* tired?

'Well, you know what Tershie's like when he's home,' she said wearily. 'He wants to make the most of his stopovers and he's not satisfied unless he gives everything one hundred per cent of his attention – including me.'

'Yes, but think of all the calories it will burn off. If it weren't for Sergei I'd probably be the shape of a dumpling by now because God knows it's the only exercise I take apart from the odd stroll along the beach, or round a garden.'

'We could try his SergeiYoga classes again,' she suggested and I gave her a look of total disbelief. *She* may have forgotten the agonies of discovering muscles you never even thought you had, but I certainly still remember, and I haven't got the figure for Lycra anyway.

Three

Of Mice and Men

NOVELTINA LITERARY AND
CRITICAL AGENCY
Mudlark Cottage, The Harbour, Shrimphaven.

Dear Honoria Snibley,
I have now had a chance to glance at your manuscript, Clacton Stole My Heart, *although, as I did try and point out at the party, I can only do a full critique on receipt of your cheque for three hundred pounds. I enclose an information sheet regarding the manuscript assessment service I offer should you wish to proceed with this.*
One or two things immediately struck me about your novel (apart from the style being a strange blend of Bill Bryson crossed with Barbara Cartland), the major one being that it contains no dialogue whatsoever. Reporting what your characters have said afterwards is not quite the same as having them actually say it, which gives more immediacy to the narrative.
Should you decide to have your novel critiqued,

34

could you please submit it double-spaced, with all the paragraphs indented, and in much bigger type?

You will find your manuscript in the porch any time you wish to collect it. I hope you have recovered from the sad loss of poor Fluffy.

Yours sincerely,
Tina Devino

I may be the last woman in the country not to be connected to the Internet, but my computer is so old that Jackie's daughter, Mel, says it should be in a museum and she hadn't realized there *was* anything earlier than Windows 95 and there was no way it could handle emails.

Only I get attached to things and we do have a history together – I remember when I bought it with my first decent book advance. It was new and exciting and the white monitor was *really* trendy, they usually came in a used-chewing gum colour ... so when did it turn that strange yellow, as if it had jaundice? I mean, it's not like I've ever smoked, so it's not nicotine.

But anyway, the poor thing is slowly dying, it's got Computer Alzheimer's and gets muddled, and it's just no good to a professional writer, that sort of thing, especially when everyone, even Linny, is emailing away like mad.

In fact, it was seeing Tertius's new computer last time I visited Linny that made my mind up to do something about it, because it was see-through and looked as if it had been sculpted from ice – quite beautiful, totally desirable, but horrendously expensive and way out of my league – but it got me thinking, and never let it be said that Tina Devino isn't at the cutting edge of *anything*.

So finally I accepted I'd have to get a proper computer as I told this really nice man that I ran into down at the Frog and Bubble at lunchtime, where I'd gone with Jackie for a drink. He just happened to have one he didn't need – brand new, with a flat screen monitor too – so of course I said I'd have it.

Jackie tried to put me off, because she said computers emitted negative energy and wouldn't do my karma any good, but I said not keeping up with technology wasn't doing my karma much good either, because editors expected you to email your books to them these days and I was starting to look like an antique. She's older than me though, the hippy generation, so it's amazing that Mel turned out such a technobabe that she thinks the only way of surfing is with a mouse in your hand.

Anyway, I got the money out on the way home, because he'd promised to drop the computer off later at my cottage, and I was walking up the street thinking that I had better get a new keyboard, and maybe a mouse too, when I came face to face with one in the pet-shop window, sitting staring at me through the bars of its cage – a *real* mouse, that is, all white and pink like the sugar ones I dimly recalled finding at the bottom of my Christmas stocking in the days when I still had a mother...

Well, before I knew what I was doing, I was in the shop parting with even more money, but something just came over me and anyway, she's so terribly sweet that I'm sure she's going to be a great inspiration.

It's amazing how much stuff one little mouse needs to keep it happy – I staggered home with two huge carrier bags and one very small, perforated box. By the time I had her cage and nest all nicely arranged and had installed her in it, the nice man from the pub had arrived and dropped off my new computer and monitor, and he was so kind he insisted on carrying them up to my little study under the eaves, before going off with the cash, whistling.

Jackie's daughter Mel just came round to help me set up my new computer, and she brought me a keyboard and mouse she doesn't want any more. When I told her how much my new computer cost she said it was *hot*, and I said I thought it was pretty trendy myself, actually, and what should I do with my old one?

'I'll advertise it on eBay for you – it's such an antique bit of junk there's bound to be someone out there mad enough to buy it ... and is that a *live* mouse you've got over there?'

'Yes, that's Minnie. Your mother said the new computers gave off tons of negative energy and would damage my karma, so I thought if I got a mouse and it suddenly keeled over, like canaries used to do in mines, I'd know she was right.'

'Are you serious?' she asked, looking at me nervously, though I don't know why because her mother is the one with the mad-as-a-hatter ideas.

'No, I'm just joking, Mel. The mouse was an impulse buy. Do you like rodents?'

'I should do ... have you seen Mum's latest boyfriend?'

'No, but my ex-husband was a bit of a handsome love-rat. Jackie's got better taste – whatever they may look like, all her men are pleasantly ineffectual.'

When we had set everything up I was totally baffled by this Vista thing, so am having to *pay* Mel to give me lessons, and so far I still only understand the bits I need to pen my immortal prose, although we are about to move on to the esoteric world of emails and the Internet soon. I won't need any of the other stuff it does anyway, which seems to be such a waste, and I wished it would all go away and make my life simpler.

Minnie watched every session from the front of her cage, gripping the bars with her little pink fingers – or paws, or whatever you want to call them – and looked like she understood it *much* better than I did.

Linny called and told me she's never visiting the cottage again unless I got rid of the rodent.

'Yes,' I said, 'but there are rodents and rodents. I was telling Mel earlier about Tim the love-rat! Minnie is different, you should see her peeling a sunflower seed, like a countess peeling a peach.'

Linny said she felt sick, but then she's never been an animal lover. Beats me why she chose to marry Tertius the Tycoon, because he's so hairy he doesn't really need clothing to be decent in public, which is probably where the word *hirsute* came from in the first place.

But she was feeling a bit snippy anyway, because she hasn't heard a thing from any of the publishers she sent her manuscript to, though I keep telling her these things take time, especially without an agent. I didn't mention the towering slush piles of unread novels – I didn't want to depress her further.

On Thursday I was sitting in my local bookshop signing hardback copies of *Spring Breezes* – well, I say *signing* copies, but you know how it is; I had three friends round me all pretending they were big fans of my books.

Anyway, there I was, when in walked this thin, peevish woman with grey hair who looked like an escaped dishmop from Cold Comfort Farm and she waltzed right up to me and said: 'Is it any good, then?' while riffling through it, crumpling the pages.

Something came over me and before I could stop myself I'd said, 'No, it's rubbish, don't waste your money.'

'All right then, I won't.' She put it down, then stared at me and said, 'I'm going to write a novel when I retire, a bestseller.'

She said it accusingly, like it might be my fault, so I told her when I retired I was going to be a brain surgeon. 'You've left it a bit late, haven't you?' she remarked, and walked off.

Really, it makes you wonder if book signings are worth the effort, doesn't it? Still, the bookshop is very supportive of local authors, despite stocking very little fiction, and actually it is called Necromancer's Nook and the decor is a bit gloomy, but the staff are friendly once you get past the vampire-style make-up. In fact, the only time I took Sergei in there I thought I'd never get him out again.

I arranged lots of local promotion for *Spring Breezes* because I've learned from bitter experience that if I wait for Libby Garnett at Salubrious to do anything about it then I'll wait for ever, and I'm trying to get a bit of a 'buzz' going about the book before the paperback comes out.

Despite all that, I must crack on with my new novel, *Dark, Passionate Earth*, now I've mastered the basics of the new computer. I simply *have* to make it big with this one, I can't go on scrimping and saving for the rest of my life, and despite my policy of attending every literary event I can beg, borrow or steal a ticket for, hovering on the fringes, hoping that some of the magic fairy dust of Instant Bestsellerdom will rub off on my wings, I don't seem to be getting any further.

Salubrious Press will probably give my next book a publicity budget of about a fiver as usual, whereas if I were a bestselling novelist they'd be pouring thousands into it, when it would sell anyway. But so it is in the world of writing: I mean, the people who win huge book prizes are usually bestsellers who

41

are already so loaded they don't actually need it ... and come to that, they're so ungrateful. If they win the Orange Prize, half the time they say they don't see themselves as a *woman* novelist, or, if the award is the Romantic Novel of the Year, they say they're not a *romantic* novelist at all. Though they still pocket the cheque anyway in front of hundreds of women who would admit to being *anything* for a bit of publicity and a fat cheque, and pardon me for the sour grapes but my cash flow is more of a thin gluey trickle lately.

Then this morning bright and early I had a phone call from a friend in publishing and she said, 'Don't look now, but your editor at Salubrious Press has just decided to "resign" and she's being replaced by a "suit"!'

'But Ruperta can't go,' I said incredulously. 'She loves my books and she *believes* in me, and I know I haven't made them much money yet, although I sell more hardbacks than most of their *literary* novelists so you can't really call me a *midlist* author, but I'm sure this next one will be a big breakthrough novel – and what do you mean, "suit"?'

'Tina, Ruperta's being replaced by a man from the marketing department, so cost-cutting might be on the agenda and midlist heads will definitely roll – and maybe one or two others,' she added hastily, but I wasn't fooled and I can see she thinks I'm up for the chop.

No sooner had she put the phone down than someone rang me from Salubrious and told me that there had been a change in the editorial staff due to *unavoidable restructuring*, and my new editor would like to meet me, and what about Friday at eleven? So I assumed big surprise and said I would, yes, and if it's Friday at eleven I expect the Suit will take me to the little Italian restaurant round the corner like Ruperta always did and I can make an impression on him so he won't even *think* of losing me.

And actually, I think him suggesting the meeting so quickly bodes well, don't you? But I can't think *what* to wear that combines Professional Woman with I'll Do Anything to Stay Published.

Four

I Believe in Miracle

The Ramblings,
Bosson Surcoat,
Cresney

Dear Ms Devino,
  I do not yet seem to have heard from you about my thriller Banking On It, *even though it has been three weeks since I sent it. (And I note that the cheque has been cashed.)*
  I would therefore like to remind you that with a topical work of this type time is of the essence, and I would be grateful if you could get back to me as soon as convenient.
  Yours sincerely,
  Harold Snaith, ACA

On the Monday, Sergei commented on how distracted I was – by which he meant I was not paying enough sympathetic attention to his latest interesting medical symptoms. I told him I felt nervous about my forthcoming meeting at Salubrious, but I am not sure he quite grasped the importance of my making a good impression on the Suit.

In fact, I found it hard to concentrate on anything else that week, though I had a ticket to a literary lunch at a very grand hotel on the Thursday, which I was looking forward to because I knew several of the novelists who would be there and I could pick up the gossip about Salubrious Press and also maybe find out where Ruperta has gone to.

But the literary lunch turned out to be a bit of a let-down, actually, because they'd put me right at the back near the loos, and I couldn't see any of my friends, and there was this tall, skinny photographer who kept running up and down in front of the table, hunched double like a mad stork, trying to get good shots of the guest speaker ... and where was I? Oh, yes – well, there was a man from an *important* newspaper on my left and someone's boring relative on my right, and finally the man from the newspaper looked at me and I smiled, as you do, and he said, 'Are you a novelist?'

'Yes, I'm Tina Devino, author of several scintillating sex 'n' gardening novels,' I began eagerly, never one to let a publicity opportunity go for want of trying. 'My new one, *Spring Breezes*, has just come out, and it's—'

'Yes, but isn't there anyone *important* sitting at this table?' he interrupted rudely.

As you can imagine, I was absolutely delirious with pleasure when the icing sugar on his Snowy Heart Meringue with Strawberry Coulis went up his nostril so he looked like he'd been snorting something and gone a bit far.

The next day I turned up at Salubrious Press on the dot, wearing a well-cut dark suit with a short – but not too short – skirt, something frivolous and low cut underneath it, and killer heels.

Normally I conduct a mild flirtation with the elderly man on the front desk while waiting for Ruperta, but today everyone seemed subdued. This little red-haired girl collected me – she seemed to be wearing a knotted hankie over one shoulder and a small paint-splattered bandage round her hips, but I expect it is very *cutting edge* – and whisked me straight up to what used to be Ruperta's office, only it looked subtly different already, though there was nothing subtle about the shock it gave me to find out that the Suit sitting behind the desk (*and* he didn't get up) was my ex-husband, Tim.

I hadn't seen him this close up for years, he having been an early mistake tried on for size and briskly discarded in Sergei's favour, so it

46

took me a moment to take it in.

Sitting down uninvited I just stared at him, thinking that he looked a lot better when he had hair.

'Well, Tina,' he said, with a cold smile. 'Glad you could make it – I know your little secretarial jobs take up a lot of time.'

My spine suddenly went all rigid and my mental faculties returned with a *whoosh*. 'You know very well I've always been a writer, and just used to temp when I needed the money, which luckily hasn't been necessary since my first contract with Salubrious.' And I didn't mention my little lit crit thingy, which just about keeps my head above the waves financially, because it is none of his business.

'You surprise me. We don't pay our midlist authors very much and I'd have thought you would have trouble living off your advances. You certainly don't seem to have done much more than earned them out, so there can't have been a great deal in the way of royalties on the sales of your books.'

He shuffled some papers together as though my entire life history was written down in front of him, which for all I know it was because he's *that* weird, and then he gave me the cold smile again. 'But I suppose you're still shacked-up with that old ballet dancer, even though current rumour says it's *boys* he's more interested in than girls – what was his name?'

And I said coolly that his name was Sergei Popov, as he knew very well, and that I had never lived with him but always preferred my independence, although we were still *together*, so clearly rumour lied.

Then I added that I didn't consider myself a midlist author anyway, and Ruperta had always thought highly of me, and he said, in a mock-sad sort of way that made me want to strangle him, that Ruperta's judgement hadn't always proved a financially sound bet for Salubrious, and now she had resigned he'd found things in a bit of a mess.

Well, we batted the conversation to and fro like this for quite a while, each trying to score points, but the gist was that if my next novel, *Dark, Passionate Earth*, wasn't (a) delivered right on time, and (b) a mega bestseller, they wouldn't be taking up the option on the one after that, because hordes of bright young writers were panting at my heels.

When I said they'd have to be fast to catch me, he said insincerely that despite our past differences he hoped that we would still be able to work together to the furtherance of the aims of Salubrious Press, or something like that – I was a bit punch-drunk by this point.

I can understand a threat as well as the next woman, though, even when it's delivered with a smile, and it is clear to me that *Dark, Passionate Earth* will sink or swim on its own: not only will it *not* get a publicity budget, but it will be lucky to make it into Salubrious Press's back catalogue.

Then Tim said he'd been glad of this chat with me and though he was very busy, which he was *sure* I would understand, Jinni would love to take me out to lunch, and in came the little red-haired girl on cue, so either she was listening or telepathic.

To add the final insult she'd been given a miserly budget to take me to Pret a Manger rather than Garibaldi's, and the most I could do was eat as many expensive sandwiches and pastries as possible, while she watched me anxiously over her lo-fat lo-cal Lettuce Carnival, so I will probably come out in spots tomorrow.

Linny was not terribly sympathetic, because she said at least I had an agent and a publisher, whereas she hadn't heard a thing about her manuscripts, which were probably being used as loo paper all over the city as we spoke due to the fine quality of the paper she printed them on in order to make them look more attractive. But she has always had money and so does not understand the desperation of someone who makes her sole precarious living from writing in one way or another ... which reminded me I had a little backlog of Noveltina manuscripts to catch up with over the weekend, too.

I had to wait until Monday to phone my agent, Miracle Threaple (whose real name is Marianne), since she doesn't encourage weekend calls even in extremis, but once I got her on the line she extracted every last word and nuance from my meeting with Tim.

'What am I going to do, Miracle?' I demanded, and she said she'd have to think about it all, but she'd call me back after Christmas and we'd get together and discuss it, and then she rang off.

I didn't feel very comforted by this, but I am putting my faith in her to think of something.

It was mid-morning before I got to Sergei's flat and due to an overactive imagination he was convinced I had been involved in some ghastly accident and was practically penning my eulogy.

After I finally succeeded in convincing him that it was really me and not my sorrowful shade come to bid him a fond farewell, we exchanged Christmas gifts, cards and possibly some strange and fatal virus that he's convinced he is harbouring.

He doesn't actually celebrate Christmas until January the seventh for some inscrutably Russian reason, but he loves presents and so do I, but I also love surprises so, however tempted, I will not open mine until Christmas morning. (And let us hope it is something suitable for revealing to the Devino family circle, among whom I will be unwrapping it.)

NOVELTINA LITERARY AND CRITICAL AGENCY
Mudlark Cottage, The Harbour, Shrimphaven.

Dear Mr Snaith,

Thank you for your recent communication, which as it happens arrived just as I was parcelling up your manuscript to return to you, together with the enclosed critical assessment. It has taken far longer than expected due to the fact that at 350,000 words it is more than twice the 150,000 paid for, and I would be delighted to receive a further cheque for the second half.

It is a very interesting work, but has some major problems to overcome in order to render it more appealing to an editor – and indeed, to a reader – foremost among them that it is too long for one novel and should be divided into two as indicated in my critique.

You will also find that by creating chapters and indenting the first word of each new paragraph, you will make a world of difference to its appearance.

For a thriller, it's not really very thrilling, is it? And I don't find all those nubile twenty-somethings throwing themselves into bed with your hero, Conrad Kravatsky, very convincing, since you describe him as a sixty-year-old balding accountant with a rather – dare I say it? – bland personality and a strong interest in golf. And what did you mean by asking me if you should increase the romantic element? There is no romantic element.

As to the alien abduction on page 545, I think that is a definite mistake, as are the passages of rather low Carry-On style comedy involving foreign nationals that occur randomly from time to time, but basically it is the sheer length of the thing as it stands that is rather too much, so that by page 500 I was losing the will to live. I sincerely think that your readers will prefer something shorter, especially if they are slow readers and have to support the weight of the book for any time, and also you might like to consider the publisher, who may well feel that the brilliance of your work does not quite justify the enormous expense of such a huge volume.

I hope you find my enclosed critique helpful, and await your additional cheque of three hundred pounds.

Yours sincerely,
Tina Devino

I packed the last of the manuscripts off on

the Tuesday afternoon before reluctantly packing myself off for another Devino family Christmas in all its ghastly splendour, leaving Minnie in the care of Mel, together with a little present of festive rodent treats (for Minnie – Mel prefers hard cash).

Oh, the things we do for love.

Five

Decimated

The Ramblings,
Bosson Surcoat,
Cresney

Dear Ms Devino,
    I have now read your comments and it is clear to me that you are incapable of appreciating a work of the magnitude of Banking On It, *and indeed, have advertised your services under false pretences. It is not my policy to throw good money after bad, so do not expect to receive any further cheques from me.*
    As to length, I can only point out the many, many blockbuster novels abounding on the shelves of airport bookshops, many of which are by famous authors who have 'crossed genres' as you put it, several times in the same book, so your advice to stick to one genre is also short-sighted in the extreme.
    As to breaking the manuscript up into chapters and indenting paragraphs, obviously this was merely a rough draft and these very minor points

have been addressed in the final rewrite.

What I was hoping to receive from you was information to enable me to present Banking On It *in a way that would draw the attention of publishers to its unique qualities, and you have failed me most dismally. Your contention that no publisher would be interested in it in its present form is ridiculous: why, the merest glance at newspapers and magazines shows that there are many, many publishing houses crying out for new writers, and clearly I should be targeting these smaller firms rather than the bigger ones, who evidently receive so many manuscripts that they cannot perceive the true gem among the dross.*

Should your conscience by now be troubling you, you could return the first payment for services you so signally failed to deliver. I will not be recommending you to my many friends and acquaintances.

Yours sincerely,
Harold Snaith, ACA

I saw Tube Man this morning on my way to Miracle's office, which is around the corner from the Ritz, and it took me by surprise to see him somewhere other than on the tube. Our eyes met – and his are like warm treacle – and we both smiled as people do when they half-recognize each other, but can't remember where from, which at least means *he* has noticed *me* as well as the other way around. Unfortunately we'd passed each other by the time I'd realized that he was Tube Man, and by the time I had turned round, he had vanished into the crowd, or the Ritz, or back into my subconscious, or *somewhere*.

I walked on thinking about the sort of inspiring things glimpses of my Heathcliff of the Northern Line usually make me think of: the strong, thrusting stems of lilies, the soft, velvety petals of pansies, silky pussy willow buds and dangly catkins ... all qualities the male interest in my latest novel has in spades. Now, there's a man who knows his dibble from his trug! I went all D.H. Lawrence for a minute, walked right past the brass plate that said Miracle Threaple Literary Agency, and then had to retrace my steps.

As I got to the door a novelist I know slightly, another of Miracle's clients, came hurtling down the steps and stood looking at me a bit wild-eyed and with her jacket buttons done up wrongly. 'Hello, Ria!' I said, and she groaned and said in a tone of utmost despair: 'Not you *too*, Tina!'

Then she turned and more or less threw herself into the nearest taxi on top of a surprised businessman, so obviously she was having a bad day, and probably her sales figures were *way* down.

Miracle's secretary and right-hand woman, Chrissy, showed me straight into her office, which is pretty swish, really. Miracle used to work from home in Hampstead until she had the run of luck with a series of three blonde-babe one-hit-wonder novelists, though that *entire generation* can't be naturally blonde, so I think the makers of Born Blonde and the like should be suing for a cut of the takings. Or perhaps I'm getting a fixation about it, and being unfair to the fair?

I was hopeful that Miracle had come up with a strategy to deal with Tim the Suit – maybe even a way of making Salubrious Press promote my next book – but she was pretty occupied on the phone when I first went in, and just waved me to my usual chair while Chrissy went for coffee.

'Yes, lovely,' she was saying, puckering up her small mouth in a way that reminded me of cats' bottoms, which they will insist on showing you while you are stroking them as if it was some special honour they are bestowing on you. Maybe in cat language it is.

'The photo shoot tomorrow and then the main article in the Sunday paper,' cooed Miracle. 'And then ... no, don't worry about writing the rest of the book yet, just concentrate on generating a bit of publicity now ... No, I know a few sentences on the back of an envelope will take some time to work up into a decent-sized novel, but I'm sure you can do it in no time, a natural writer like you. Yes, I was surprised at the size of the advance too, but I'm sure the book will deserve it and soon earn it out ... Mmm, yes, wonderful. Yes, lovely. Yes, of course ... bye...'

Miracle put the phone down with a long sigh, then let her expression of bright eagerness lapse into exhausted exhilaration. 'I only hope I don't end up half-ghosting the book like the last one, but at least the family connections mean mega publicity, and anyway, who cares if she's another one-hit wonder, so long as the hit is *big* enough!'

'Another blonde-babe-bombshell first-time novelist?' I asked gloomily.

She nodded. 'Yes, that makes five in a row. I thought when I had the first three one after the other – boom! boom! boom! – things couldn't get much better than that, but now I feel like all my cards are turning up aces, my slot machines all bells – ding, dang, dong—'

'I get the idea,' I said, interrupting her hastily. She was capable of going on like this for hours and I was not exactly in the mood to hear other authors' praises sung. But of course, while I may *resent* the huge advances, at least I am not too insane with jealousy to realize that she is doing so well out of them that she can afford to have a few more writers who don't make her quite so much – like me. Or anyway, that was *my* theory.

Miracle was looking serious again and not quite meeting my eyes over the coffee cups, which considering how long we've known each other was a pretty bad omen. 'How is the next book coming along?'

'Oh, fine – nearly finished. I'm just polishing now. But, Miracle, have you thought about how to deal with Tim? It's been worrying me no end, because—'

'Well, that's just it,' she broke in. 'I *have* spoken to Tim – in fact, he's the editor who has just taken on Lydia, the girl I was talking to – and *that's* the way he envisages Salubrious Press going.'

I stared at her, puzzled. 'What do you mean, Miracle? That they are only taking on the Lydias from now on?'

'More than that, I'm afraid – they don't want *any* midlist authors at all, just established bestselling ones and new first-timers, and all the publicity budget will go there.'

'But – but I'm under contract! I mean, the next one, and the *option*—'

'Oh, the next one will be published, but they won't take you up on your option on the one after that unless *Dark, Passionate Earth* does amazingly well, and since they aren't going to spend anything on promoting it, that's rather unlikely, isn't it?'

There was a small silence while I gazed at her, stunned, and she gazed back at me with an air of sweet, sad reason on her broad-cheeked Persian cat face. 'Of course, you may just find another publisher, but the market is difficult and although you sell well, you don't sell *huge* amounts. But the fact is that even before this happened I'd decided to make some changes.'

'Changes?' I echoed stupidly. I was beginning to think I'd left my brain at home in Shrimphaven – or even my body: could this just be a nightmare?

'Yes, I'm taking on so many new authors that I've decided to follow the example of some of my colleagues in the business, by dropping the ten of my authors each year who are performing least well, to make room for the new ones ... and I've already seen the other nine.'

'The other ... *Miracle*!'

'Well, Tina, it's very, very sad after all this time, I know, but I'm afraid after *Dark, Passionate Earth* I will have to let you go, though I will, of course, continue to represent you for any rights from your first novels. And I can recommend you to another agent if you can find one who is still taking on authors.'

I opened my mouth – to plead I admit – but all that came out was a strange, frog-like rasping noise and there is never a prince in sight to kiss and make it better when you most want one.

'You may well find that a change of agents is quite invigorating to your writing, even,' she suggested, smiling encouragingly.

And I might well find myself temping again.

'And so I don't have an agent, and soon I won't have a publisher either,' I told Linny when we met in Liberty's café afterwards. Though really I was in such a state of shock that even shopping wouldn't help me and after tea and buns we got in a taxi and went back to her place.

Tershie was home, and he was *terribly* sweet and opened champagne, and even offered to send me all the way home by taxi, which I declined because naturally I always hope to see Tube Man, and anyway it would be phenomenally expensive even though Tershie can afford it, and I don't like to take advantage of my friendship with his wife.

Speaking of which, once I'd calmed down a bit and had two glasses of bubbly I realized that Linny, although sympathetic as always, was also sort of enjoying the situation too, but I suppose that is perfectly natural since our friendship is built on mutual regard: I'm jealous of her because (a) Tershie is super-rich and (b) hardly ever home so (c) Linny doesn't actually have to do anything at all except shop and pretend to write novels. In return, Linny is jealous of me because (a) I'm published and (b) she fancies the leotard off Sergei.

Well, after a while I decided that I'd have to devote the whole of the foreseeable future to polishing up the new novel, which is due in a week on Friday, and making sure it's mega-bestseller quality, then trying to think of a way of getting publicity that wouldn't cause my arrest on indecency charges, though I do have *ages* before it's published in December to come up with something.

So I decided to take in Sergei's flat on the way home, and leave him a note saying I couldn't see him on Monday due to pressure of work, though actually I secretly hoped he would be there to give me a bit of *comfort*, despite it being the time when he would normally be overseeing one of his Sergei Yoga classes.

But as it turned out, it would have been better if I *hadn't* wished that, because when I was at the furthest end of his street I saw this tallish, dark-haired man come out of his front door, and although I couldn't make out who it was, Sergei followed and kissed him on both cheeks ... though he does that to practically everybody so it doesn't really mean anything; but he doesn't usually follow it up with a back-thumping embrace.

There was just *something* about the tableau that made me turn on my heel and head for the nearest tube station. If anything *is* going on, I simply can't take it at the moment, and I'm not even going to *think* about it, and anyway, Sergei's never shown any inclinations the other way that I've noticed.

Of course by the time I got home I realized I was being stupid and over-imaginative due to the shock of Miracle's bombshell, and knew that if I casually mentioned Sergei's visitor to him, he would tell me who it was straight away, all perfectly innocently. Not that Sergei ever *looks* innocent, because his natural expression can only be described as *impertinent*, an old-fashioned word, but entirely apt in his case, probably something to do with the winged eyebrows and high cheekbones. Cheeky just isn't the same at all.

I tried to call him but his phone was out of order, so I phoned Linny instead and she said she'd be delighted to go round with a note for me saying I would be working too hard next week to see him, and I said not to get her hopes up because he was fully occupied, and anyway, did not fancy big bossy cows, and she laughed.

But we were just joking, and she wouldn't actually really have a fling with him, even if she had the opportunity, because not only is she my best friend, she's always been totally faithful to Tershie – and anyway, Sergei's met her a couple of times in the Lemonia with me and there was no sexual chemistry that I could see even though he does like bosomy brunettes.

You know, I've been mulling over the way all the midlist authors are being dropped by the big publishing houses, and I think there may be a couple of drawbacks they haven't thought of.

For instance, what happens when the old bestselling novelists (like Hereward Bruns-wick, who gave Miracle her nickname and is still her star author client) die or hang up their laptops? I mean, most novelists work up to bestsellerdom over a few years, they don't just spring fully-formed out of no-where.

And although a few of the one-hit wonders will go on to develop into good authors, most of them will vanish, because no matter how huge their marketing budget if the actual book is crap the book-buying public are not going to be blowing their money on the next one, are they?

Still, who cares what I think? Certainly not Tim the Suit.

Or, it seems, Miracle.

NOVELTINA LITERARY AND CRITICAL AGENCY
Mudlark Cottage, The Harbour, Shrimphaven.

Dear Mr Snaith,

Thank you for your letter. I am sorry that you don't feel you have received good value for your money, as I have many testimonials from other authors thanking me for my sage advice. However, I have still spent a considerable amount of time working on your manuscript and so, not only will I not be returning your cheque, but I enclose a bill for the extra 200,000 words.

With regard to your comments on switching genres several times within a novel, yes, there are indeed several famous authors who have done it – and that is the point: they are famous, they have made their name, and simply because of that they will be published and their books read whatever they write. When you are equally famous you can do the same, but until that glorious day dawns I suggest you try and limit yourself to one genre.

Now, a word of warning about these 'small publishing houses' that you mentioned intending to target with your magnum opus: they are all vanity publishers, and you will be expected to contribute financially if you wish to see your book in print. Non-vanity publishers are so inundated with unsolicited manuscripts that they have no need to advertise for more!

I hope this timely word of warning will be helpful to you, and I look forward to receiving your cheque for three hundred pounds.

Yours sincerely,
Tina Devino

Six

Affiliations

Dear Tony,

Just to say a belated thank you for another memorable Christmas. I am entirely panettoned out.

Sorry I had to rush away, but as I explained, not only did I have a heap of manuscripts waiting for their critiques, I also had to see my agent and promote my new paperback, Spring Breezes. *The latter job is even more important now because my agent has dropped me, and if* Spring Breezes *isn't a mega-success so will my publishers.*

I must say, considering that by now we only have about a teaspoon of diluted Italian blood in our veins, you are sounding more and more like something out of The Godfather, *Tony, and I'm sure poor Mary would much prefer her given name than Maria, which is terribly* Sound of Music, *let alone inflicting Bruno, Dino and Fabia on your unsuspecting children's heads – though actually, come to think of it, there are worse names you could have chosen and the boys do seem to like theirs even if they sound strange in a Welsh accent.*

I quite understand your interest in tracing your ancestry like that American book Roots, *and commend your attempt to learn Italian at your age, but frankly I feel suddenly assuming a broken Italian accent makes you look slightly ridiculous, so please don't carry your identity crisis to extremes, will you?*

Oh, and another hint – ditch the shades when you are indoors.

Give my love to Mary and the children.

Your affectionate sister,

Tina

I have spent almost the whole of the last ten days working my butt off on the new novel, and feel I've added a whole new layer to its rich compost heap. So now maybe Miracle will change her mind when she sees it. And Tim will regret his words to me when he reads my wonderful prose ... and pigs will be flying backwards over Shrimphaven.

To look on the good side, the day after Miracle gave me the chop Sergei sent me a lovely bouquet of thrusting great lilies with a *deeply* sympathetic and encouraging message regarding my writing situation, not to mention a rather nasty slur on Tim's parentage and sexual prowess – or lack of it – so clearly Linny caught him at home and told him *all.*

It was so terribly comforting knowing he cared that I entirely forgot to ask about his visitor when his phone was fixed and he began ringing me again, but I am sure it doesn't matter.

Thanks to Mel's lessons I am now quite used to my computer, but which pervert programmed the spellcheck facility? It takes my perfectly innocent English words and tries to substitute the most peculiar – not to mention *obscene* – words, and it definitely has an *oral* fixation. It did cross my mind to wonder what a novel would be like if I accepted all its suggestions and maybe I will try that sometime and see what happens?

But certainly, now I have access to the Internet, it has opened up a whole new if strange world. It's also opened up a second postbag every day, with all those emails to answer, some of them a little odd to say the least.

Where do they get my email address?

From: *tinadevino@mortalruin.com*

Dear Mr Ndonga,
    Thank you for your recent email. I can't imagine how you got my address, even though, as you say, we are fellow writers with friends in common – although you don't say which. I am terribly sorry to hear of all the difficulties and persecutions you

faced in your native country, and certainly the very second I can manage it I intend to join PEN: and this brings me to the crux of the matter, in that I cannot possibly afford to credit your bank account with any amount let alone the sum you mentioned, for as you know, novelists are either bestselling or scraping along, and I unfortunately fall into the second category, as presumably do you. (By the way, I could not find you on the Amazon site under Ndonga – do you use a pen name?)

Sorry I can't help financially, but good luck with your future writing,

T. Devino

I dispatched my novel to Miracle on the Thursday by courier instead of delivering it myself as I usually do, but I didn't feel like facing her until she'd read it, and frankly I was exhausted, absolutely *drained*, and so it was quite late when I checked my calendar and emails and stuff and realized that I was supposed to be going to this writers' meeting next day, one that might be useful.

My career clearly needs all the help it can get at the moment, so despite being completely wrung out I girded my loins and set out.

It was the first regional meeting of the Affiliated Authors to be held in Shrimphaven, though why they needed a regional meeting so close to London baffled me, until I walked behind the scenes at the museum and realized that most of the members present hadn't got enough miles left on the clock to get to the Great Smoke and back.

Anyway, after due consideration of the options I sat next to this lively-looking woman with the aisle on the other side for escape if necessary before Battle of the Zimmermen commenced at tea and bickies time.

She looked at me and then smiled, 'Aren't you Tina Devino?'

I admitted modestly that I was, and then she said her mother-in-law adored my books, she was such a keen gardener, and she herself loved the way I drew parallels between plants and sex. 'I'm Ramona Gullet, by the way – I write dark psychological suspense.'

'You are? Then I've heard of you, too!' I exclaimed. 'Someone from Women for Intellectual Advancement tried to get me to speak to them recently, and said you'd given them a brilliant talk.'

She shuddered. 'Oh God, it was absolutely awful! That dreadful woman just bullied me into it, and then they all sat around afterwards picking my novels to pieces and being patronizing! *And* I did it for nothing.'

'Thank goodness I got out of that one,' I said.

71

'Well, it was good copy, so I did manage to get something out of it – I used the experience in my new book, *Blood on the Table*.'

'Did you? I'll pop into Necromancer's Nook on my way home and see if they've got a copy.'

The panel came on and we had to hush up while this dismal earwig of a man told us all about his little publishing house, which was in fact so small that not only had I never *heard* of it; I expect you have to have a map reference to find it at all and even sat nav won't do you any good. In any case they only publish really cutting-edge poetry, and we all know how big the audience for *that* is.

Then it was the turn of the haggard black-haired woman who'd clearly drawn herself the huge crimson lips that nature hadn't given her over her own thin lizardy ones. She told us how she'd had a mega success with her non-fiction book: *S & M: A Complete History*, but somehow no publisher wanted her brilliant first novel, *Slapping the Leather*, and so she'd had to resort to self-publication. Now it was selling like hot cakes, she bet the publishers were all kicking themselves.

Well, whatever turns them on.

After that, the man from the Affiliated Authors thanked them both and said what an interesting contribution they'd made by telling us about their experiences, and then asked if anyone had any questions.

And boy did they! I kid you not, I think more than three-quarters of that audience were self-published, and the first man's question summed it all up when he said that he sympathized with the second speaker because no publisher had taken his *History of Newts in Little Botting with Hand-drawn Illustrations*, although he knew personally that there was a huge market out there for it and all his friends thought it a work of genius.

Where have I heard that line before?

'In the end I had to publish it myself,' he said in aggrieved tones, 'and I've still got five thousand copies in the garage because selling them myself is proving exceedingly time-consuming and since I can't garage the car and those old Hillman Imps can be temperamental if you leave them outside in winter, it's very inconvenient ... and why on earth won't booksellers stock self-published books like mine?'

'Because there isn't a big enough market for books about newts in Little Botting to make it worth their while, dimwit,' was obviously the only reply. 'Or any of the other minority-interest books and strangely attenuated novels the rest of you have had printed.'

But no, the small press man and the haggard harpy and the Affiliated man, who was very kind in a well-meaning way, earnestly discussed this at length and I thought they'd never shut up.

But finally they had to call a halt and it was tea and bickies time. Ramona and I looked at each other and with one accord escaped outside and went for a stiff drink at the Frog and Bubble, and she is really nice, so one good thing came out of the dismal session anyway, and next time I go to a London meeting of the Affiliated Authors (which are not at all like this one), at least I will know one person because she goes to them all.

Dear Tony,

While I was, of course, very sorry to hear that Father O'Donovan suffered some sort of mental crisis over Christmas and has now gone away on a six-month retreat to find himself, I can assure you that it was nothing to do with me.

Yes, I did have a conversation with him at your Christmas Eve party, but we discussed plants, flowers and books, all perfectly innocently – he is a very keen gardener, isn't he? – and he asked *me for a copy of one of my novels, I didn't force it on him.*

Actually, Snapped Blooms, *being one of my earlier books published before Salubrious Press asked me to spice things up a little, has rather less scenes of a sexual nature than my recent ones, and also I sent a note with it pointing out which pages he ought to avoid in view of his vows of celibacy, so he didn't have any carnal thoughts thrust upon him, as it were, though it was all good wholesome earthiness: I don't do bad sex.*

Honestly, you'd think I was an embodiment of the Antichrist the way you go on!

Tina

Seven

Flat

The Ramblings,
Bosson Surcoat,
Cresney

Dear Ms Devino,
I write firstly to inform you that I have no intention of sending you any further undeserved sums of money, and should you persist in your demands I will put the matter in the hands of my solicitor who will know how to deal with you.

Secondly, I am delighted to say that, no thanks to you, Ripplit Publishing has accepted my novel **Banking On It** *and it will appear later this year in a two-volume edition. You were wrong about small firms who advertised for manuscripts all being vanity publishers, for I am not paying them one penny apart from a contribution to the costs of production, which I will easily recoup from sales, for they inform me that they send promotional material to every single bookseller in the country! I enclose a photocopy of their glowing appraisal and* *acceptance of my work in the hopes that it may be a lesson to you.*

Yours sincerely,
Harold Snaith, ACA

NOVELTINA LITERARY AND CRITICAL AGENCY
Mudlark Cottage, The Harbour, Shrimphaven.

Dear Mr Snaith,
Thank you for your interesting letter, and the enclosed copy of the book acceptance by Ripplit Press.

I also note your refusal to pay me for the work I have done, but despite this I certainly wish you all the success you deserve, and indeed, under the auspices of Ripplit Press I am confident that you will receive everything due to your particular genius.

Might I suggest that you join the Affiliated Authors Group? They are always looking out for new novelists of your calibre, and at their regional meetings you will find many, many kindred spirits.

Sincerely yours,
Tina Devino

Sergei was in an unusually tender and affectionate mood on the Monday, full of schemes for promoting my next book, all of them highly imaginative but all, unfortunately, equally impractical.

Much of our conversation was carried out with him lying on the wooden floor for the sake of his back, which had been giving warning twinges. He once badly strained it lifting a too-heavy ballerina, which led to him having to leave the Royal Ballet – but don't get him started on *that* grievance! In any case, the pursuit of health and fitness led him to develop his own exercise routine, which has been lucrative.

After a while I arranged a couple of sofa cushions alongside so we were at least at the same level while we talked and could hold hands and, occasionally, kiss…

I remembered something I was going to ask him and casually mentioned that I'd passed the end of his street after my meeting with Miracle while he was seeing a friend off, but had been too upset after what had just happened to come and say hello. Luckily he didn't question why I should be in his part of town at all if I wasn't coming to his flat, but instead *immediately* said he wished I *had* called in, because his guest had only been Grigor.

'You remember Grigor, don't you, Tsarina? I took you to one of his first performances.'

'Oh, yes,' I said, relieved because Grigor has been rather Sergei's protégé since he arrived on the British ballet scene, and he is a tall, dark young man, albeit weak in the chin (but clearly not the *knees* or he wouldn't be able to lift all those ballerinas about like so much thistledown).

After a while Sergei said he thought his back was fine, the twinges had been a false alarm, and got up again, but he still seemed more interested in consoling and encouraging me than our usual pursuits (*pursuits* being the operative word on an energetic day), and so we walked round to the Lemonia for lunch.

We saw Linny across the room with a couple of her Rich Bitch local friends, but although she waved she didn't beckon us over to join her, which was thoughtful of her as I could see the other women at her table all urging her to, though it certainly wasn't *me* they wanted to get their acrylic nail extensions on.

But they were out of luck, because Sergei was tenderly seating me at a table for two and divesting me of my coat as though unveiling something terribly beautiful and precious, which was very endearing when the room was full of much younger, prettier and *thinner* women than me.

'Now I have you to myself, Tsarina!' he said, all gleaming, liquid dark eyes, beautifully moulded lips and flashing teeth – a bit Valentino and slightly manic, but then, when is he not? And I thought he'd had me to himself all morning, but I didn't say anything because he can be quite thrillingly sheikhish like this sometimes, and actually I rather like it.

Then while we ate he asked me all kinds of things about Miracle, contracts and publishers and stuff, which he hasn't seemed very interested in before, but I am sure it was all meant to show me he really cared. He hung on my every word. I'd never known him quite so un-self-absorbed and he even offered to drive me back to Shrimphaven afterwards, though I tactfully declined because he drives in a series of thrusting leaps, much the way he dances, and I'm not sure the rest of the road users are quite au fait with ballet moves.

I roughed out a whole chapter on the train back, despite being seated by a serial crisp eater, and arrived home to find that my paperback author copies of *Spring Breezes* had finally arrived.

And soon after that the *Shrimphaven and District Gazette* called to do an on-the-phone interview, which they are going to run with a picture of me they keep on file (I am big in Shrimphaven), so there is *one* source of publicity at least, and a small drop in the ocean though it might be, I almost feel like a real author.

★ ★ ★

This big arts centre about fifty miles away asked me if I would like to go and do a novel-writing workshop for their Literary Society, all keen writers, two and a half hours all about myself and getting published and so on, so clearly my fame is spreading faster than manure, and when they said they would give me a hundred and fifty pounds how could I say no? God knows I need the money now and will have to do this sort of thing full-time if I don't have a bestseller with *Dark, Passionate Earth* or find another publisher (and agent), so I agreed.

And at least I *am* a novelist, because half the writing workshops in the country are taken by people who've never had work published, unless by themselves, or they've been published in a totally different field to the one they are actually teaching, talk about the blind leading the blind: speaking of which, did I ever tell you about the time I was asked to go to a centre for the visually impaired and do a talk? No? Well, they were almost all (a) extremely old, (b) had just had lunch, (c) were most of them deaf as posts and (d) wanted to go to sleep; so after shouting out the first paragraph I'd prepared about my novels, which seemed to send them off quite nicely, I just walked about telling funny stories to the few who were awake, and after about half an hour most of them came alive again and we had a really *exciting* discussion about Stephen King, whom they all adored.

But I digress: so off I went to the Whimpergreen Foundation Arts Centre with my talk all prepared – one I've done successfully all over the place – with worksheets and discussion ideas and all the rest, and I was supposed to be met in the cafe beforehand and given lunch by Luella somebody – it might have been Whimpergreen? In which case clearly this is a family-founded thing, and if it was a business don't they call that sort of thing *nepotism*?

She proved to be a stocky, belligerent-looking woman with little piggy eyes who met me with the accusing words: 'So you're the Romantic Novelist, are you?'

I said, 'Guilty as charged,' smiled sweetly and added, 'But I can assure you there are more than one of us, though thank you for the compliment.'

She looked a bit gobsmacked, and so was I when I discovered I had to buy my *own* cafeteria-style lunch, which is not quite what I was expecting, though it was very good if pies are your forte.

Luella sat on the far side of the table with her arms crossed, studying me as if I was a low form of plant life, which was not good for the appetite.

Then to top it all, this deaf old bat sidled up, plonked her tray down next to me and started whispering on and on about some novel she'd written, and said she was sure I would want to read the synopsis and first chapters over lunch so that I could discuss it with her at the meeting.

And I said no, I'd rather just eat, and I wasn't going to discuss individual manuscripts, but my talk was about how to write a novel that sells, which I'm sure she would find very relevant.

At this heresy there was an audible intake of breath from Luella and several other people sitting around earwigging, then they all rose up and surrounded me like a posse and led me into a back room. It was dark and gloomy, with a sparse selection of hard chairs and a Formica table, and I thought they were just going to incarcerate me in there and go away, but it turned out that this was where the Literary Society held its meetings.

So they all sat round the table and looked at me expectantly and I waited for Luella to introduce me ... and waited.

She was slumped in her seat picking at the skin around her fingernails, but after about a year and a half she looked up and said brusquely, 'Tina Devino. I expect she will tell you all about herself.' Then she folded her arms and looked *unamused* like Queen Victoria crossed with the Empress of Blandings.

Well, never has two and a half hours gone so slowly, although that particular workshop usually *overruns*, especially with questions and answers and worksheets, but I'd hardly even got into it before Luella started fidgeting, sighing, rolling her eyes and muttering things like, 'Get on with it!' and 'I thought you were going to tell us how to write a novel!' and stuff like that. Then she flatly *refused* to do the questionnaire I handed round, which usually breaks the ice and gets everyone bonded and talking.

When it got to her turn to answer she said she never read books and wasn't interested in them and she couldn't remember ever writing *anything*, and what was the point of all this? Really, she was just a great, glowering black hole in the room, sucking everyone else's creativity and enthusiasm into it, and clearly she intimidated the life out of them for it was like getting blood out of a stone to get them to say anything.

To lighten things up I made a little joke about Devino being a good name for a writer, because having a name near the beginning of the alphabet meant you were usually on the first couple of bookshop shelves nearest the door, and that was *it* – a red rag to bully Luella. Clearly, being

Whimpergreen and the last one to be called for anything in school has rankled all her life, though I should think no one *would* have picked her anyway if she had always looked like that.

Then she tossed her pencil down so hard it ricocheted off the table and nearly hit the woman opposite, who had to duck. Luella said she wasn't getting *anything* from the session and it was a *complete* waste of her valuable time and stormed out leaving this nasty silence.

I struggled on, but due to non-participation I'd run through my stuff like greased lightning and was starting to lose the will to live, but anyway I carried on with the last bit, all about how to aim a book towards a particular market slot for the best chance of success, and then they woke up and got all puckered round the mouth, and were going: 'Oh no, no, no! We couldn't *possibly* write a novel aimed at a market, we have to write what is *in* us.' And: 'We don't write for the money, only for art's sake.'

I nearly asked them if they thought that Charles Dickens was just writing for art's sake, or whether he might possibly have had one eye on the market and the other on the money, but I didn't want to lose my life over it and honestly some of them were starting to give me the evil eye in a very Wicker Man kind of way, though that might have been the fluorescent light strip. And just when did some novelists start going all precious about what they were writing, as if we weren't all ladling different bits of stew out of the same pot and trying to live on it?

But of course *they* were all writing Great Literary Novels that the public would jump on with glad cries because they were so *brilliant*, and the inference was that I was only a *hack* capable of writing cheap little potboilers, and never read anything more literary than Mills and Boon, and because they'd pre-categorized me as a romantic novelist who of course are all (a) the same and (b) bad.

So I said, 'Have any of you actually *read* one of my novels?' None of them had, or any of 'that kind of thing'.

I tell you, it was a bundle of laughs all the way through, and except for needing the money I would have left at coffee time because I felt I was beating against a closed door, not to mention being patronized by a lot of amateurs.

And to top it all, Luella came back in, although she didn't say anything, so I don't know what for except to scupper any faint empathy that might have sneaked into the group in her absence.

When I looked at my watch to see how far

time had dragged its weary carcass, she said: 'Is that *it*, then?'

Then two people said they had to dash for the bus and just left, so there was no vote of thanks at the end. Everyone else straggled out and Luella sighed and said I might as well follow her to the front desk and she would pay me, so I did, and she clearly didn't think I was worth it and she was being done.

I took the money – goodness knows I worked for it – but I'm never ever going back there even if they offer to pay me double and hang banners out.

Though, actually, I don't suppose they *will* ask me because I'm clearly not what they had in mind, and maybe they should have checked with Little Ms Assertive from Women For Intellectual Advancement; *she'd* have put them right.

Eight

Vintage Chic

NOVELTINA LITERARY AND
CRITICAL AGENCY
Mudlark Cottage, The Harbour, Shrimphaven.

Dear Ms Pucklington,
   No, I am sure we have never met since I am an invalid and rarely leave my home – indeed I discourage all personal callers since I need absolute quiet for my nerves. So although it is most kind of you to offer to call and discuss the more esoteric aspects of your novel in person with me, you can see it is quite impossible.
   Also, I am afraid you have confused me with the novelist Tina Devino, who is a distant family relation. (I am told that her novels are absolutely brilliant!)
   It is certainly very surprising that your first novel, Slapping the Leather, *was not snapped up by a publisher, so that you had to print it yourself, especially in view of the success your non-fiction book on the history of sex and masochism had earlier achieved, and I will look forward to reading*

your new novel Beyond Rubber *to see if I can put my finger on any problems that may be holding you back from acceptance.*

If you wish to proceed, please post the manuscript to me including a cheque for the full amount (made out to T. Devino) and include a stamped, addressed envelope for its return.

Yours sincerely,
Tina Devino

I saw Tube Man again today on my way to Linny's – the first time since we passed outside Miracle's office – and we exchanged smiles, and his dark eyes turn *down* at the outside corners and his smile makes me want to *cry* ... and my God, he's certainly Tube Man in more ways than one and I suddenly felt a yearning to have mine *untied* or I would if they were tied, but you know what I mean. (This is unusual: I have never been able to see the *point* of children and, having been orphaned so early, the concept of motherhood is a foreign country to me.)

Unfortunately, Tube Man was getting on as I was getting off, but surely that means he must live in this area of London? Why haven't I seen him hanging out at the Lemonia or any of the coffee shops or Russian tea rooms? And if I'd been in the possession of my senses I'd have got right back on the train with him!

I wonder what he does for a living. 'One thing's for sure,' I said to Linny, 'he's not a writer. Have you noticed how there aren't any good-looking male writers, only female ones, though why they all have to be blonde beats me? But male writers are never really tasty, or if there are any I haven't seen them yet.'

'What about Martin Amis?' she suggested.

'What about him? He's not *ugly*, but would you want to see him across the breakfast table?'

Actually, the only stunningly attractive writer I can recall to mind is Ted Hughes in his pre-grizzled days, when, going by the photos, he would have done it for *me*, that's all I can say. He certainly seems to have put it about a bit, so had I been born a few years earlier who knows what might have happened had our paths crossed? It would have had to have been pre-Plath, though, since I have been programmed by my upbringing to leave married men well alone, on the strict understanding that hell would have a special place put by for me if I didn't.

But on second thoughts that would mean I was even older than I am now, and my God, I think I'm going into deep denial! I've been thirty-five for so many years now even I can see that the lie is straining at the bonds of credibility and truthfully I'm not so much the shady side, as that dark spot in the corner that the sun never reaches.

NOVELTINA LITERARY AND CRITICAL AGENCY
Mudlark Cottage, The Harbour, Shrimphaven.

Dear Ms Mendosa,
  Thank you for your recent enquiry. Yes, the Good Lord must have guided you to pick up that old copy of the Writers' & Artists' Yearbook *with my address in it, while visiting your English friend in St Lucia. He moves in mysterious ways.*

  Your novel sounds very interesting, based as it is on your deprived and brutal childhood in Cuba, but I am afraid that I cannot receive it through email, even as an attachment. I would imagine it would be much cheaper for you to approach one of the many agencies in the USA, but if you have definitely made your mind up that NOVELTINA is the agency for you, then perhaps I could simply send you the critique without returning your manuscript, thus saving you return postage.

  I am unable to glance at it first and give you an idea of its saleability, as you suggest, without payment.

  Should you wish to proceed, perhaps your bank could advise you on the correct way to forward the full fee to me at the same time as the manuscript.

  Yours sincerely,
  Tina Devino

Tomorrow is one of the Society For Women Writing Romance get-togethers in London, which I usually go to, though sometimes I sneak off to meetings of the League of Romance Writers, the rival outfit, where I have several friends and they will let anyone in at the door if they sub up a few quid.

Don't ask me why there has to be two rival groups of romantic novelists, because the reason for the schism goes back to some argument lost in the mists of time, when apparently there was such a heated discussion that it was practically drawn fountain pens at dawn and one faction flounced off to start up their own association, which I hadn't realized until after I'd joined the SFWWR; and though we often attend the same literary events it can be a bit *West Side Story* sometimes, because we don't actually mix but eye each other over our wine glasses from opposite ends of the room, while trying to guess whose party dress came from M & S and who had gone down the vintage chic route (usually me).

Anyway, next day found me at the SFWWR meeting and there were a lot more men there than usual, most of them looking a little *weird*, so I said to Freya Rample that perhaps romance was in the air, and were they all spouses and significant others?

And she said no, they'd had a sudden influx of male members due to amending the constitution at the last AGM so that Rule 14 now reads: 'All men applying to become members shall, if qualified for acceptance (see Rule 13 of the Constitution of the SFWWR), henceforth be honorary women for the purposes of membership.'

Only at this point I'm afraid that schoolgirl giggles got the better of me, and every time dear Freya's puzzled and slightly enquiring gaze rested on me during the ensuing meeting they broke out again, and eventually I just had to leave early and go home before the stewed coffee and rich mixed biscuits.

So I never actually got to talk to any of the honorary hermaphrodites, but they were probably mobbed at the end for their novelty value anyway so I wouldn't have got anywhere near them: several of the female members are much bigger than I am.

Still, it gives me a future pleasure to look forward to.

Truth is stranger than fiction.

Nine

Insalubrious

Dear Tony,

No, I don't think there is any market for a book about the Devino family history, even if you threw in bogus Mafia connections and the Ice-cream Wars of the early years.

You are really getting into this family research thing, aren't you? Let me know if you find anything juicy as I might get some publicity out of it. And you could write the book just for yourself (and the family) to read, couldn't you?

Anyway, I hope you get this before you fly off to Italy on a pilgrimage to the village of our forefathers, from which our family was so brutally torn by poverty and expediency, as you rather graphically put it, because I distinctly remember Granny telling me once that it had been shrugged off the mountainside by Nature years ago.

With love to all the family,
Tina

Sergei has gone back to being abstracted,

and Linny frankly has gone totally off the rails, all giggly and frenetic and eating way too many chocolates.

Their expressions of concern for my career seemed to have been short-lived too, even when I told them about the day I finally phoned Miracle to ask what she thought of *Dark, Passionate Earth*, only to have her say casually: 'Oh, I didn't read it – Chrissy had a quick look and said it was the usual stuff then sent it on to Salubrious.'

So now I await the verdict from Tiger Tim. What if he isn't Suited? What if he asks for huge, impossible changes? What if he says the *whole thing* needs rewriting?

Tertius told Linny last week that if she doesn't lose a stone quickly he's going to divorce her, because it's important in his position for his wife to look elegant, and how can she look elegant when she's got more spare tyres than Kwik-Fit? Also, he's booked her in for laser treatment for her facial hair as a birthday present.

Well, I do keep telling her about that, but she just says it's her Lebanese blood, and in hot countries it's thought quite sexy really and anyway, she can't stand the thought of having it lasered because she is sure it would hurt.

I said, 'Not as much as your husband

divorcing you would, not even childbirth could hurt that much, though maybe having your nose hair waxed would run it a pretty close second. How are you going to lose the weight *quickly*?'

'I'm going to restrict my diet to apples, crackers and Camembert and nothing else, then I don't have to worry about calories, or carbs or anything.'

'Don't you think you might get pretty sick of apples, crackers and cheese?'

'Yes,' she said brightly, 'but if I go off them, I'll lose even more weight, won't I?'

I suppose it's no unhealthier than a lot of the diets touted about, and at least she isn't going to starve to death even if she stops eating as she's carrying enough body fat to keep her going for at least six months, if not longer, mostly around the middle, so she looks as if she's wearing one of those inflatable swimming rings under her clothes.

She did already look a bit thinner when I visited her to see how the first laser treatment went, but she'd made an excuse and phoned up to postpone it, she is such a big coward.

Then as we sat down there was this house-rocking subterranean thundering and I said to her, 'Linny, I didn't know the tube ran under your house. Funny I've never noticed it before, isn't it?'

'It doesn't,' she said, looking self-conscious, and that's when I realized it was just abdominal rumblings and wondered whether Tershie would really *prefer* living with a thin bald camel to a plump sleek walrus?

NOVELTINA LITERARY AND CRITICAL AGENCY
Mudlark Cottage, The Harbour, Shrimphaven.

Dear Ms Mendosa,

Thank you for your manuscript Voice Of The Mangrove, *and the bundle of notes. East Caribbean dollars are quite colourful, aren't they? I don't think my little bank in Shrimphaven had ever seen any before, and it took them ages to work out the transfer rate.*

I have now read your novel (which wasn't easy, due to the ultra-thin paper and the fact that it was single-spaced, though I do understand about the weight being an issue when you are posting it from abroad).

Yes, I can quite see that your life experience is just as valid as Isabel Allende's, although I think your manuscript is reading rather too much like an autobiography at the moment.

But I'm sure readers will sympathize with your heroine, Maria, as she struggles to better herself, even when at sixteen she marries that rich old American, Jerome, in order to escape Cuba.

97

While I expect that the later episode set on Antigua – where on a complete impulse she suddenly pushes him down a blowhole and escapes into a new life with the insurance money – is entirely fictional, I think you will have to make poor Jerome a bit more than just fat and old in order to get your readers to feel that his demise was justified at this point.

Apart from these minor quibbles, which I have expanded on at more length in the enclosed critique, I also wondered why you had chosen to write in English when your first language is so clearly Spanish.

I am not saying that your English isn't absolutely brilliant, considering, but there is quite a large market for novels in Spanish, and if it were a success then it would probably be translated later. Just a suggestion – I mean, it may be worth trying a Spanish version first.

Anyway, I hope you find my critique helpful.

With best wishes for your success,

Tina Devino

A *Guardian* review for *Spring Breezes*! It said it was a 'subtle blend of gardening and eroticism'.

Well, I do my best.

I sent copies of it to Miracle, Tim the Suit and Libby Garnett, the Salubrious marketing person, just in case they missed it.

Jackie's daughter Mel, who has been giving

me the computer lessons (and also mouse-sitting when I am away), pointed out to me that compulsively visiting my book page at Amazon is not so much surfing as dabbling my feet in the smaller waves. So she has now shown me how to access Google and other search engines, where I found hundreds of mentions of *me*! OK, perhaps that's a slight exaggeration, but lots anyhow. Only it is just like opening Pandora's box and I can't resist checking all the time to see if anyone has said something new (and flattering) about me...

On the Amazon site there were some new readers' reviews of my books, and one woman said she and her husband had always been keen gardeners, but my novels had changed their lives, but she didn't say whether for better or worse. Another one said she had now read *all* my novels and was indescribably appalled by my depraved and warped view of sweet innocent nature, though goodness knows there is nothing innocent about nature that *I've* ever noticed. But apart from these two, all the reviews are unambiguously enthusiastic.

My email address book is still pitifully small and it's mostly just Linny who fills my inbox, with the odd missive from Salubrious or Miracle and though Mel says if I went on Facebook I would soon have lots of friends, there are friends and friends, aren't there?

Mel's definition of 'friend' seems pretty loose – but then, her mother's is even looser, so I suppose it isn't surprising. Mel's now writing a novel too, which she is reading to me in very short chapters, and I can see it is actually just a day-by-day description of what it is like to live with an ageing upper-class hippie with a good accent and connections, a series of dodgy boyfriends, and just enough private income to keep you one tin of beans above the poverty line.

Ten

Hot Beds

NOVELTINA LITERARY AND
CRITICAL AGENCY
Mudlark Cottage, The Harbour, Shrimphaven.

Dear Ms Pucklington,
 What an interesting novel Beyond Rubber *is! I feel I have learned so much, although I did become somewhat lost in one or two places, especially about the feather, and the role of the bicycle pump ... so perhaps the general reader might also find these references a little baffling.*

 However, I think you will find a publisher for this and your lack of success to date has simply been because you have been aiming at the wrong market.

 Instead of Mills and Boon you should try the publishers Red Hot Candy, since they are always gagging for this sort of thing and – a major point – do not require any plot whatsoever between erotic scenes, which will suit your excellent novel perfectly.

 Therefore I enclose my critique to enable you to

101

add that final polish to your work, and a copy letter for you to send to Red Hot Candy Press together with your manuscript.

I wish you all the best in successfully placing it.
Best wishes,
Tina Devino

I was in the papers again today, because the *Sun* had an article about me! Well, actually it was about Sergei *really*, but it mentioned me.

There was a very unflattering photo of him leaving the stage door of the Royal Ballet with his arm around Grigor, under the caption, 'Is Sexy Sergei a Dancing Queen?' Under it: ' "Absolutely not!" says close friend Tina Devino, author of several sizzling sex 'n' gardening novels.'

When they called me yesterday for my comments, they promised to mention my books and so they have; they are also going to review *Spring Breezes* and offer six copies to the first readers who write in, so my profile is going up and up! Anyway, I was happy to set them straight about Sergei.

Of course when Sergei rang me, incandescently furious with the *Sun*, I sympathized with him no end, and he was actually *grateful* that I had defended him like that in print, so I didn't mention my ulterior motives.

But of course I would have defended him anyway, because I know his affectionate and hands-on disposition and just because Nureyev seems to have been a bit AC/DC it does *not* follow as the night the day that all male ballet dancers are.

He does seem very fond of Grigor though.

Probably as a direct result of all the recent publicity, my new book seems to be selling well if my Amazon ratings are anything to go by. And people keep phoning me up and asking me to *do* things, most of which I refuse because I have started on the next novel, so far untitled, even though I don't yet know if I still have a publisher and I haven't found another agent, despite writing to several. They are all 'going to get back to me'.

Reminds me of the letters I used to receive with my rejected novels before I got published, that always said they'd enjoyed reading my work but it was 'not quite for them'.

Still, last night found me addressing my local writing group, which may not sound very exciting (or lucrative) but they all buy my books in hardback and it doesn't do to neglect your roots, does it? (Which reminds me that mine are showing, and I must buy a bottle of Naturally Mine hair colour in Dark Rich Nigella on my way to Waitrose later.)

During the question and answer bit at the end of my talk the chairwoman, who looks like a testosterone-laden Oxo cube on legs, stood up and said pretty belligerently: 'It's all right for *you*, writing salacious froth about nothing much! But what about the market for religious poetry, that's what I'd like to know? Publishers won't touch it, even though it's straight from the heart and I've had *countless* personal tributes from people who have been privileged to hear me read it.'

So I said there was a bit of a limited market for religious poetry, except possibly in America, where the market was naturally bigger for *everything* because there were lots more people over there, but I didn't personally know much about the USA book scene.

'Have you even *been* there?' she demanded.

'Only once, a few years ago.'

'Then I am surprised you didn't explore all the publishing opportunities while you were there.'

I said I'd been more interested in exploring the *shopping* opportunities at the time, and then she said I was a light woman.

Someone from the back called out: 'Oh, shut up, Enid, we love her books!' and several voices said, 'Hear, hear!'

Enid swung round, eyes narrowed. 'Who said that?'

Things might have got nasty if a pocket-sized ex-colonel type hadn't got up and given me a hasty vote of thanks and declared it tea and sticky buns time.

Libby Garnett phoned to say that since I seemed to be getting some publicity for *Spring Breezes* (no thanks to her, I might have said, but restrained myself), would I like to do a little book-signing tour of London?

'Do you mean signing stock, like I did with my first Salubrious novel, *Bad Seed*?' I asked, and she said yes, because there wasn't much call for sit-down author signings these days except by bestselling novelists.

She doesn't know about Necromancer's Nook, where I sit down very comfortably at a table with a glass of blood-red wine at my elbow and *lots* of people come, even if they are my friends.

But I *am* prepared to do *anything* to promote my novels, and anyway, if I sign lots and lots of books at least it means they can't send them back to the publisher, so the bookshops will make a push to sell them ... perhaps. So we settled on Thursday and Friday.

She emailed me an itinerary, and just as I remembered from last time the bookshops were all over the place, involving much backtracking and tube journeying.

I stayed over in Linny's palatial guest suite,

since she'd volunteered to come with me again, though I bet she wished she hadn't when the weather turned cold, rainy and dismal.

Well, we visited six bookshops in quick succession, and each one went much the same: a slightly scrofulous young man met us, led me to the designated spot – usually standing at the corner of the cash desk, or on the edge of a prominent book display (someone else's) – and left me with a pen and a pile of virgin copies of *Spring Breezes*.

I signed them all with a flowing 'Best Wishes – Tina Devino' and then we girded up our Burberrys and went on to the next.

We were exhausted by the end of the first day, and my wrist hurt, my feet ached, and I'd forgotten how to spell my name. But the next one went much better after Linny insisted on going by taxi everywhere (she paid), and the day started with a signing at Harrods where they were *delightful*, giving me a comfy chair and a nice pen and one of those 'signed by the author at Harrods' bands that they put around the books.

We ended later that afternoon at Selfridges, where someone actually asked me to sign a copy she was buying, and by that time Linny was wearing the Harrods 'signed by the author' band paperclipped into a tiara, drunk on the smell of new books.

When we got home Tershie had come back from whatever moving and shaking he'd been doing and insisted on taking us out to dinner at the Ivy, where he frequently seems able to magic a table up at short notice. He is so kind, rich, and away such a lot that I told Linny that husbands don't come much better than that, if you have to have one at all, which I don't, but if Salubrious *do* dump me I might soon be in the market for something similar.

NOVELTINA LITERARY AND CRITICAL AGENCY
Mudlark Cottage, The Harbour, Shrimphaven.

Dear Neville Strudwick,
  Thank you for your manuscript, Sons of the Soil, *and the cheque.*
  Yes, I am *Tina Devino the novelist, and I'm so glad you enjoy reading my books.*
  No, surprising as it may seem, I don't have a huge garden myself – the tiniest seaside pebble and driftwood garden, in fact – but I love visiting gardens and adore flowers, so don't find the research part of my novels at all difficult.
  I look forward to reading your novel.
  Yours sincerely,
  Tina Devino

I am having a website made! No longer am I a dinosaur, but firmly into the twenty-first century, and Minnie the mouse is proud of me. She is my little mascot, and worth her weight in sunflower seeds and Mousienibs the Rodent Fitfood.

I saw an advert for someone who specializes in creating author websites and rang up, and this really nice young man came out to see me, but I had to give him back, they wouldn't let me keep him.

He is going to put these links on the net, like Sexy Flowers and Hot Beds and all the details and covers of my books, and my reviews ... and then I will have even *more* mentions on Google! Hurray!

Just heard from Salubrious about *Dark, Passionate Earth* – but not from Tim the Suit, just that little anxious-looking girl who took me to lunch. Jinni, was it? Anyway, she said it just needed a little tweaking here and there, nothing much, and was I happy to let her do it? Only they had decided to bring publication day forward to June in both hardback and paperback, so it was going to be a bit tight.

So I said yes, it certainly was! And my previous books had always come out in hardback just in time for Christmas and paperback early the following spring, like the aptly named *Spring Breezes*, and why were they changing that?

'It's a *managerial* decision,' she said reverently. 'I'm just passing on the message. So it's all right for me to go ahead with the changes, is it?'

'No, it certainly isn't,' I informed her crisply. 'I want to see the whole manuscript and make any strictly necessary changes myself.'

She'd obviously been told to avoid this at all costs, but she wasn't up to the job because there's no way I'm letting that happen. So the upshot was that the manuscript with notes arrived by motorcycle courier not much more than two hours later, and it was just as well I insisted because the copy editor had changed all my half-French hero's dialogue, which I had written with the merest *hint* of an accent, to something farcically ''Allo 'Allo, zis is 'ow you are saying I am loving you, cherie?' style.

And as if that wasn't enough, several of the sexier paragraphs had been totally rewritten in the style of Tiger Tim, a novelist manqué, and not to their improvement either.

So I just made the minor *sensible* changes they asked for and then phoned Tim (after a battle with Jinni) and told him straight out that if he rewrote any part of the book I would demand that my name be taken off it and then tell the press, with whom I was *very* well in just now, exactly why he was doing this to me!

Tim backed down right away, as you would if faced with a tigress guarding her cub – and believe you me, *no* novelist likes to have anyone else rewrite their words, let alone their ex-husband! He said he'd just thought the changes an improvement, but he would not insist on them, and he was glad to see I'd *finally* been given some publicity after all this time.

Then he suddenly said he had to go, and I could hear poor Jinni bleating in the background so it looked like she was up for sacrificial goat.

Flown by a triumphant adrenaline surge I phoned Miracle, who was 'too busy to come to the phone' according to Chrissy, so I outlined to her what I'd done, and she said, 'Go, girl!' in her warm and enthusiastically American way, and I nearly asked her what the market for religious poetry was like in her native milieu and then thought it would just muddy the situation.

NOVELTINA LITERARY AND
CRITICAL AGENCY
Mudlark Cottage, The Harbour, Shrimphaven.

Dear Angie Heartsease,

No, it doesn't surprise me in the least that fairies guided you to choose my agency out of all the others, because one of my closest friends will not now perform any action, no matter how everyday, without a protracted if silent negotiation with her guardian angels.

However, I am afraid your little friends were wrong on one point: I still have to charge you the full amount for reading and assessing your manuscript, even though you are *a single mother eking out a living selling fairy-inspired craft items at a tented encampment in mid-Wales, because this is how I make my living.*

There is another possibility, though, since the brochure of craftwork made by your commune that you included was most interesting, especially page three: the hand-beaded, handkerchief-hemmed Midsummer Night's Dream gossamer skirt in Titania Blue, should you happen to have one in size eight, would be perfectly acceptable payment for my services, and I would not require the matching wings.

Let me know if we can come to some agreement.
Yours sincerely,
Tina Devino

My computer keeps telling me I'm performing an illegal action as if I'd hacked into the Pentagon or something, which I haven't as far as I know, though how could I possibly *tell*? I don't suppose a little sign comes up saying 'welcome to the Pentagon', does it? I wonder how hackers know where they are.

But it certainly wasn't *helpful* to tell me it was an illegal act when I didn't even want to do it – I was only trying to find yet more exciting mentions on the Internet of wonderful *me*.

Who *are* these machines to try and boss me about anyway? I mean, who programs them to interfere in innocent people's lives? Next thing they'll be telling me to stop talking to my Dictaphone so much and do some work!

Eleven

Don't Stop Me Now

NOVELTINA LITERARY AND
CRITICAL AGENCY
Mudlark Cottage, The Harbour, Shrimphaven.

Dear Neville Strudwick,
I was more than happy to sign the copy of Spring
Breezes *you sent me, especially since you enclosed*
return postage. I'm so glad you enjoyed it even
though your wife Glenda found it a trifle too risqué
for her taste; but, as you say, a shared love of nature
makes a strong bond.
Yes, the photo on the back is fairly recent, but I
am afraid it is terribly flattering – I assure you the
reality is far different!
I will get back to you about your manuscript,
Sons of the Soil, *in the near future.*
Yours sincerely,
Tina Devino

Although it wasn't Monday, it was Valentine's Day, so I made the trek up to Sergei's

flat carrying a huge plastic sack of crinkled tissue-paper roses made by Jackie, who has been compulsively making paper flowers since the early seventies and doesn't know what to do with them.

When I moved to Shrimphaven the first thing I did was join the local library, but to do it I had to fight my way through a crinkled jungle of foliage to where Jackie sat at her desk like an ageing Pre-Raphaelite Sleeping Beauty. I came out with her phone number, three good murder mystery novels and a giant sheaf of bright orange paper poppies.

When Sergei returned from the Royal Ballet, where a couple of times a week he puts a select few through their pliés and pirouettes, I knew he would appreciate a bank of ruby-red roses leading to his door and a big, glossy, over-the-top card on the mat.

I was glad I didn't see Tube Man en route because there's nothing elegant about carrying black plastic bin bags about, but actually I was later setting out than I'd meant to be and so it was well after the commuting rush and into quiet mid-morning time when I approached and stood looking down through Sergei's windows.

He'd left a light on and the wooden shutters were not quite pulled across, so I could see into the flat through the airy muslin curtains ... And then – quite suddenly – something *big* in nude pink and wearing a feathered blue butterfly mask darted fast past the window and was closely, if more slowly, followed by a satyr-masked and totally naked Sergei, clearly about to get a Popov someone that was not me.

Well, the next thing I recall is standing by the little fountain in the gardens nearby, the water in the white marble shell-shaped basin beneath all covered in a mat of roses leaking red dye, like the aftermath of a watery St Valentine's Day massacre, which it was come to think of it, and then I came to my senses and made off hastily towards home before anyone caught me.

I just couldn't face even Linny just then, though why I should feel so hurt when I sort of half-suspected I wasn't the only one in Sergei's life and have just been kidding myself I was, I don't know. But seeing it in the all-too-solid flesh is something else entirely.

And yes, I know I've been mentally unfaithful to Sergei with Tube Man on several occasions, not to mention between the pages of my book with numerous sexy heroes, but none of that *counts*, does it? I don't care what anyone says, carnal thoughts are not the same as carnal goings-on.

Who *was* that woman in the butterfly

mask? (If it *was* a woman, that is, for I only noticed the mask because she – he? – was looking back over one shoulder ... and yes, *of course* it was a woman, I can't start doubting his inclinations now, even if I do have serious grounds to doubt his fidelity.)

I got home somehow, though I don't remember much about that either, except that I am sure I cried the whole way because my face looked like a red sponge in the hall mirror. I expect my fellow passengers on the train ignored my tears with true British embarrassment or perhaps nervousness engendered by my scarlet-stained hands.

In my absence my neighbour had taken delivery of a Valentine arrangement of expensive orchids, which he passed to me over the fence as I was fumbling with the door key. (My eyes were a bit swollen, so it was hard to see what I was doing.)

They were from Sergei, of course, and simply too beautiful to jump up and down on ... and in fact the whole scenario, with the roses and the unfaithfulness and the orchids and the doubts, not to mention the Lady Macbeth aspects, suddenly all clicked in my head so that I immediately dropped the novel I'd begun and started writing a new one, to be called *The Orchid Huntress*.

Even though I am agent-less and contract-less and so may not be able to sell it, I still can't stop writing, a bit like Jackie and the tissue paper flowers: it's a compulsion.

Tears dripped and blistered on the paper as I scribbled and my heart sat leadenly embalmed by betrayal in my chest – but as Miracle always used to say, 'Life's little tragedies make such good copy, dear – don't waste one agonizing second of them.'

Between frenzied bouts of scribbling (I always write the first draft longhand), alternating with hours spent crying into my pillow, I pondered various courses of action, such as phoning Sergei up and ending it, or sneaking into his flat at a time he would definitely not be there to look for clues as to who Blue Butterfly Mask was – or both.

I've still got a key from the days when Sergei had his ancient and ailing Siamese moggy, Petruschka, so that I could pop in and see how she was when he was working. I'm sure he's forgotten I have it – I rarely go there uninvited nowadays ... and look what happened when I *did*!

Is this why he's been so distracted for the last year or so? He has someone else and hasn't told me? And if so, he's kept it very dark, because no one has dropped *any* hints about it to me, though Linny is usually one of the first to pick up tasty bits of gossip, her antennae cover such a wide range...

Oh God, that makes me think of butterflies again.

But although I keep getting out and fingering the door key, I've managed to restrain myself so far. Meanwhile, the writing is very cathartic, and all my unvoiced and previously largely unacknowledged suspicions about Sergei's faithfulness have surfaced in it, forming a scummy mat across what were once the limpid depths of our love...

Excuse me while I write that down.

For a couple of days I didn't answer the phone to anyone, just checked for messages.

One of Linny's aunts was in town, and as usual she was detailed for escort duty around the shops, so I knew she would be too busy to wonder why she hadn't heard from me, but Sergei kept leaving plaintive little bulletins about his back, and how he wished he could hear the sound of my voice, and why wasn't I answering his messages? All of which I deleted.

But after much application of the twin balms of writing and common sense to my wounded heart (and cold water to my swollen eyelids), I visited Sergei as usual early on the Monday morning. (The common sense was Jackie's – she said Sergei was so gorgeous she wouldn't mind sharing him with a *harem*, and anyway, did I have anything *better* lined up? And of course I don't have *anything* lined up at all outside the pages of my novels.)

He opened the door wearing something over the top in brocade and fake fur like a Tartar prince, plus a welcoming smile, which vanished when he saw my face. Maybe the cold water and make-up hadn't been as effective as I'd thought.

'My darling! What is the matter?' he exclaimed, but I evaded his embrace and walked past him into the room where I turned to face him.

I managed to keep my cool and said straight out that I'd seen him at it (nearly) on Valentine's Day and was *deeply* hurt, but understood if he'd found someone else (or even *several* someone elses?) and hoped we could part amicably. 'And I just wish you'd told me, Sergei, because I always thought we were friends as well as lovers,' I added.

My voice, which had been remarkably steady throughout the little, dignified speech I'd prepared, suddenly wobbled all over the place and my chin probably did, too.

Despite being both startled and miffed at being found out, he made a good recovery. 'But how could you accuse me of such a thing, my Tina? You mistook what was happening. It was my therapist – my back was so bad and—'

'Oh, pull the other one, it's got bells on it,' I snapped, which puzzled him rather, though he definitely took on board the total disbelief bit.

He changed tack and became terribly passionate in his flamboyant way, throwing himself at my feet and crying: 'It was nothing but a regrettable impulse of the moment, my lovely Tsarina, not the beautiful thing we have between us!' and much, much more of the same kind of stuff, though he refused to say who the butterfly was except that she was nothing compared with me, his beautiful Tina.

He should have thought of that at the time.

'It was not important ... I barely remember what happened. I had perhaps one glass of good Russian vodka when I got back from the Royal Ballet and—'

That explained a lot. 'There's no such thing as good Russian vodka where you are concerned, Sergei,' I said shortly. 'You *promised* me you wouldn't drink it any more after what happened last time a friend gave you some. And it still doesn't excuse the fact that you betrayed me.'

'Never in my heart!' he protested. 'See, I kiss your feet in abject apology, I grovel, I plead for your forgiveness and understanding, my Tina...'

I let him go on like this for a bit, since he seemed to be enjoying it even if I wasn't, then when he started to run out of steam, I said, 'Let's simply carry on as *friends* for the moment, Sergei, until I can learn to trust you again,' which I thought was a pretty good line. I wrote it down as soon as he'd gone to stoke up the samovar, and it certainly hedged my bets nicely.

So now here we are just being friends (which we were anyway) while he tries to get back in my good graces, and it is all rather restful without the sex thing which, although down to once a week at most had increased in vigour to compensate, so I probably needed a break, though if I find I miss it I will simply let him win me round later when I've forgiven him.

But don't think I'm not still feeling betrayed and deeply wounded, because I *am* and things will never be quite the same again.

Nobody's mentioned the bleeding roses.

Once her aunt had gone home I finally told Linny all about it – and I'd put it off because I thought she might be sort of pleased since she's always fancied him herself. But she was actually terribly sympathetic and insisted I repeat every single bit of the conversation with Sergei, which is what I really wanted to do anyway.

And then she said she personally was *totally* disillusioned with men, but did think that Sergei actually cared for me in his own way, and I must have known what sort of man he was but just shut my eyes to that side of things, and I said I supposed so, but what I wanted to know was whether I was special or merely part of 'that side of things'.

'Special,' she said. 'I'm sure anyone else is just – well, just *sex*, and they don't mean anything to him, and I think men like that are the pits.'

'But I thought you had the hots for Sergei?' I said, surprised.

'Only from a distance. I found him rather scary that time I took the note round for you.'

Then she blushed, so I think she still fancies him really, despite everything, and unfortunately so do I...

She also said speculation on the identity of the figure I'd glimpsed was pointless – it was probably another dancer, which sort of kept it in the family and didn't really count, and I said so long as it hadn't been Grigor, though strictly speaking he is more a leading light these days. He looks much more impressive on the stage – you don't notice the lack of chin at all when he is actually dancing.

'Don't be silly,' she said firmly. 'I've never seen anything more heterosexual than Sergei in my life, make-up or no make-up.'

'No, you're right,' I agreed. But anyway, thank God for my strong sense of self-preservation, which has led me to take a belt *and* braces approach to contraception all my life. (Or maybe it's more a dislike of babies?)

'And once I knew about the vodka it did explain things a bit, because the real Russian stuff his friends sometimes bring him back is so strong it removes the veneer of civilization like paint stripper and he turns into something a bit too primeval for my taste – and that's another promise he broke, because he swore he would never touch it again after last time. You remember? He—'

'Yes, I remember,' Linny broke in hastily. Then she suggested I just lay back and enjoyed being wooed again, because she had found from her disagreements with Tertius that this was always the fun part of a relationship, especially the little trinkets he bought her to make up.

And there may be something in that, because this morning I received a very expensive diamond-studded heart pendant with the message: 'Forgive me, Tsarina – truly you have all my heart.' And, it seemed, most of his bank balance.

The gesture had quite a softening effect on me, though I have no intention of weakening yet.

NOVELTINA LITERARY AND
CRITICAL AGENCY
Mudlark Cottage, The Harbour, Shrimphaven.

Dear Mrs Vauxhall,

Thank you for your manuscript, Frodo's Incredible Adventure, *which I have read with great interest, and also the cheque for ten pounds which, as you so rightly point out, is probably more than my asking rate if you worked it out word for word.*

Although I do take your point that novelists seem to be getting younger and younger, and agree that your granddaughter, Kylie, shows huge promise as a writer, yet I do feel that at seven it is a little early yet to think of her work being published in book form. There is also the minor difficulty of length, for I'm afraid publishers do expect slightly more than five hundred words in a novel. Also, which you may not have noticed unless you are conversant with The Lord of the Rings, *there is just a* tiny *element of plagiarism here, which is only natural, since beginning novelists are very often derivative.*

Yes, Kylie is very precocious, isn't she? Even so, just how much experience of life can you have had at seven, living in a quiet country hamlet? As you so rightly point out, so did Jane Austen, though I believe she was slightly older than seven when she wrote Pride and Prejudice.

I hope you find my comments helpful, and that

Kylie will carry on writing, and perhaps enter some of the many children's writing competitions where her very original style may well bring her success.

Yours sincerely,
Tina Devino

Twelve

Playing With My Heart

Dear Tony,
Would you please refrain from sending letters to Sergei insinuating that if he doesn't make an honest woman of your sister you will send 'the boys' round to make him an offer he can't refuse. Not only do these menacing messages profoundly puzzle him, but also even if I wanted to marry Sergei (which I don't), it certainly wouldn't be at shotgun point, especially sawn-off!
So butt out of my affairs.
Tina.
PS. Love to Mary and the children.

Today I went to an ordinary meeting of the Society For Women Writing Romance, although usually I only go to their parties and awards ceremonies – and, my God, they know how to party! – but they'd invited me to be part of a panel speaking for ten minutes on 'My Writing Technique'.

The meeting was at the Arts Club, and

Linny came too to see if she could get any tips, but we fortified ourselves with coffee at the Ritz first because I was quite nervous. I seem rather to have lost my bottle for this kind of thing since the Whimpergreen incident.

Anyway, there were five of us on the panel and I was first, so I began my little piece by describing the rituals I have to perform before I start a new book.

'For example, before I began my current novel, *The Orchid Huntress*, I first had to take a brand-new A4 lined pad and rip the front cover off and get a new black rollerball pen from the drawer. Then I lined up the little stone bear and the brass monkey (see no evil) on either side of the pad at exact right angles – though sometimes my friend Jackie sneaks in and covers my desk in good-luck objects, booby-trapped to fall off every time I walk across the floor, so I have to clear them off first, and the heart attack brought on by the sound of a huge crystal hitting the deck can't be said to be lucky, and anyway that sort of thing is much better on the window refracting little rainbows about the place, isn't it?'

I stopped for breath and the chairwoman said quickly, 'Er, thank you very much, Tina, that was very interesting.'

I hadn't actually finished but I must have

overrun my time, so I sat back and listened to all the others. They seemed to be talking more about words per page, and how much they wrote every day and stuff, though I noticed at the end that I got most of the questions and everyone wanted to tell me what they had on their desks for good luck.

Linny said she'd learned something, and why hadn't she been to one of the meetings before? Why, in fact, hadn't she *joined*, as one of their Nouveau Novelists?

'Because you've never shown any interest in meeting other writers before, and usually you're going to some much grander function whenever I ask you,' I pointed out.

She said she couldn't compromise her social position because of Tershie, but she'd try and 'network' a bit more in future whenever she could, and as she had a copy of the SFWWR membership application form in her handbag, who knows?

Linny was very jealous of my diamond heart, though goodness knows she has enough precious trinkets of her own to start a shop. I am having to wear it *everywhere*, including to bed, since anyone could break into my cottage with a bent nail file and I simply can't afford to burglar-proof it, so will just have to hope for the best and my terribly nosy neighbour, the Rottweiler of Shrimphaven.

I did once have engagement and wedding rings, but flogged them long ago to buy this really nice winter coat in a sale that has stood me in good stead for years, and I just don't think it's possible to wear cashmere out, do you?

So now I'm not so much wearing my heart on my sleeve as round my neck, and it was much admired at the SFWWR meeting.

A journalist phoned me up at the crack of dawn about some tabloid photos of which I knew *nothing* until then, so I dashed out to buy the rag. And the newsagent gave me a very *slimy* look – and oh my God! There's this series of *mercifully* fuzzy snaps of Sergei's back garden with the caption: *Sexy Sergei in Rites of Spring*, which I thought was pretty clever for a guess actually, and fortunately you couldn't make the woman out at all clearly because of the well-draped dancer.

It's just a pity the foliage wasn't that thick last year because normally Sergei's garden is like a green *cave* by May.

I managed to get Sergei on the phone just before he left for his classes and he'd already been hassled too, but said he had declined to comment except to say that he hoped his neighbours had better things to do than spy on him, let alone photograph him about his private pursuits, and one of the reporters had made a crack about pursuits that had really got his back up.

'You will deny everything, Tsarina,' he said grandly, which of course I was going to do anyway.

Then next day's spread was headlined: *Was Sergei's Nymph Write In There?* with that photo of me and Sergei coming out of the Lemonia (you know, the one with the drunken daisies?) and the article was all innuendo and speculation, though it did give 'saucy Tina's sex-romp novels' a good plug even if not in terms I would have preferred.

So the *next* time someone asked me for a comment (on the doorstep this time), I said with a Mona Lisa smile that Sergei and I shared a love of nature that drew us together, and had been dear friends for years, but I was not at liberty to divulge details of his private affairs.

It was all in the paper next day, plus the immortal cliché, which I *don't* remember saying: 'When asked if she knew the identity of the woman in the photo, Ms Devino smiled and shook her head, then said her lips were sealed...'

Later Miracle phoned me up, the first time she'd actually spoken to me since she gave me my marching orders, and said I should carry on with the enigmatic smile stuff and plugging my books, and that not only had the *Spring Breezes* promotion in the *Sun* done my sales some good, all this new scandal-raking wouldn't do me any harm either if handled the *right* way.

I wondered if she was having second thoughts about getting rid of me and soon it would be 'come back, all is forgiven'?

Don't think I'd better give up my manuscript assessment service yet, though!

NOVELTINA LITERARY AND CRITICAL AGENCY
Mudlark Cottage, The Harbour, Shrimphaven.

Dear Neville Strudwick,

I have now assessed your novel, which you will find enclosed together with your critique.

You said in your introductory letter that it was based on your own life, and actually I didn't think things were that exciting growing up in the country in the fifties, especially all the rather Zane Grey bits riding about with guns, but clearly I was wrong. The incident at nineteen when you shot and killed your twin brother Barnaby in a freak accident must have been a terrible experience, and clearly one you could never entirely forget, although when his girlfriend Glenda turned to you for comfort and eventually you married, it must have been some solace to you both.

The trouble is, apart from this one incident the

book doesn't really seem to be going anywhere, being as it is the episodic exploits of a group of young boys growing up in the country linked by a series of rather dry lectures on farming methods, and although the boys have lots of adventures, the book seems to entirely lack any kind of premise whatsoever – and, indeed, a plot – and I am afraid is not publishable as it stands.

However, I think I have discovered your true métier! Yes, I believe that if you visit your local library and take out lots of cowboy books and study them closely, you can then turn Sons of the Soil into a super Western! Take that incident with your unfortunate brother and fictionalize it into the central event of the book, making it a stirring tale of unrequited passion and love of the ranch and that kind of thing: maybe the young Glenda figure could be the only daughter of a rich rancher? Or a widow trying to run her place herself but sorely in need of a Shane-like figure to ride into her life and rescue her? You can then retitle it along the lines of Sons of the Arroyo Canyon and submit it to publishers specializing in this type of novel.

That adult computer class for beginners you attended certainly taught you a lot, and perhaps you could ask your teacher to show you the spell-check facility, which is invaluable. Also, when you do finally submit your novel to a publisher, I am sure you will not economize by printing it off on to the back of old Farmer's Union letters and *the like, but use fresh, decent-quality printer paper.*

Well, Neville, I hope you are not too disheartened by my critique but instead excited by the thought of embracing a whole new genre!

I wish you all the best with it,
Tina Devino

Today I was guest speaker at the Shrimphaven Gardening Club's annual lunch, and not only did they *pay* me, but they also gave me food and drink.

But unfortunately I can't really do justice to either before speeches because I get too nervous, so all I get out of it is a thimble of coffee and a weird mint that tastes as if it's been stored in a damp box for ten years at the end of the meal once itall over.

Afterwards, when I was earning my fee by mingling, this woman asked me where I got my inspiration from and I said off the Internet.

She said, 'Really?'

'No, I'm joking,' I confessed, 'I really get all my inspiration from Nature.'

And then she nodded darkly and said there was certainly a lot of *that* about, especially in Shrimphaven, and when I saw her later leaving she appeared to be married to a very strange and exotic specimen of it.

★ ★ ★

Guess what? I am to be one of the Brown's Bookshops' Bright New Flowers of Fiction in Spring! I realize they only bloom briefly before being replaced, but I still can't figure out why *now* after all these books, though I suppose the tabloid stuff might have swung it.

Linny said it should be Dull Old Bloom of Fiction, which I thought was a bit snippy, but then, she'd just sent another of her manuscripts off and had it back again practically by return of post. I wish she'd let me read one sometime so I could see if she's any good, but she won't.

The typeset proofs of *Dark, Passionate Earth* have come, and not only do they seem to be rushing the book towards publication at unseemly speed (probably to get rid of me quicker), but it seems they're also economizing on it, because it appears to have been typeset by someone whose native language is something other than English.

Still, you can't say that I am not professional and so I had corrected and turned the thing around to Jinni at Salubrious within three days. She emailed me instantly to say it had arrived, and to thank me for sending it back so promptly – she seems scared of me for some reason, and scared of Tiger Tim for *good* reason, so she's between a rock and a hard place, and if I'm the rock I think I'll be Blue John fluorspar because it's so *pretty*.

You know, sometimes I think getting a computer has not so much opened up a whole new world as a can of worms.

I mean, aren't emails quick? Just as you reach the end of all the answers to messages you've had piled up for days, you get the replies back, with *more* questions, and the whole thing is like some infernal cycle that never stops.

And now I've started getting rude emails from companies who pretend to be my friends so I open them, but after the first couple – and my God, were they porno-graphic! – I'm now much more cautious and delete anything that looks the least bit dodgy. Only *now* they're sending me blatant-ly obvious messages, and why target some-one called Tina with *men's* porno? *Enlarge your penis by three inches in one week?* I don't think so, thank you very much.

Must ask Mel if there is a way of getting rid of them. At least now I know what people mean by spam because I've seen it only too clearly on my screen.

I *am* having lots of what Mel calls hits on my new website, also more emails though, and I can see why that nice man who set the site up said I should have a separate email address on it instead of my own personal one, because some of the messages are very odd indeed; but then, I suppose the links are too, so I can't complain, so long as they buy the books after visiting the site.

I met Ramona Gullet for coffee at the Jolly Fisherman and she signed my copy of *Blood on the Table* and I signed *Spring Breezes* for her. We are forming a mutual admiration society, and have decided to meet like this once a month.

I told her all about my attempts to find another agent, and how Miracle seemed to be changing her mind a bit now I was having all this press coverage and *Spring Breezes* was doing well, but I had absolutely lost faith in her and if only I could find another agent who would take me on I would go anyway.

Ramona has a wonderful agent, but he only does crime and thrillers, not my kind of thing at all, though she said she would ask him if he knew any other agents who might be interested, which was kind of her.

Then we settled down for a good novelists' gossip, which is a lot of fun, and though I love Linny to bits and she *is* writing novels, until she is published and understands the whole business more we can't really have this type of conversation, which refreshes the parts non-writers can't reach and sends you back to your keyboard and mouse(es) rejuvenated.

By the time I got home, the remains of the day were an offal-coloured heap of tangled clouds on the horizon and until I managed to throw off the dark but interesting influence of Ramona's conversation, *The Orchid Huntress* took a very odd turn indeed.

Thirteen

I Should Be So Lucky

3 Underpass View,
Ringroad Way,
Birmingham

Dear Ms Devino,
I enclose my novel Shooting Up, Shooting
Down, *plus a cheque for three hundred pounds,*
although I wondered, since this is a very short
novel, whether I would receive a refund for part of
that.
As you can see from my work, I am very much
influenced by the Trainspotting *school of fiction,*
and being a social worker in Birmingham I have
certainly experienced life's rough underbelly first
hand. This is a very black, futuristic vision: a cry of
doom.
Since I am a poet, already published in many
magazines, including Strimp, Angry Young Poets
Bulletin, *and the prestigious* Cracked Voices
Journal *with my elegy, 'Meditations of the Beetle',*
it seemed a logical progression to me to write the

whole of my novel in free-verse form, an idea that I am sure will strike you as innovative and original.

My novel has been rejected by two mainstream publishers with no comments whatsoever, except that one remarked that Wilfred was a very old-fashioned name considering that I am only twenty-nine. Actually I was named after the Great War poet Wilfred Owen and certainly do not wish to change my name!

Perhaps you could advise me on who would be most likely to appreciate a work of this kind.

I look forward to your reply.

Yours sincerely,

Wilfred Quinn

I am invited to attend a photo shoot with the other five Brown's Bright New Flowers of Fiction in Spring, and there will be coverage in Sunday newspapers and a glossy mag! Then we are to tour their London branches signing books, where we will all be displayed face-out at the front of the store in a special stand, as will the books.

At least it meant that I had to tell Sergei that I couldn't make it on Monday, because it's been getting a bit tricky holding him off, especially since the diamond heart, and clearly he feels he's done the sackcloth and ashes role to death. But just because he's famous *and* gorgeous, does that really mean that he can sleep with anyone he wants and

I have to accept it because I'm the only one he loves?

I just put that question to Jackie, who looked at me as if I was a halfwit and said, 'Well, *duh*, Tina! Yes, it certainly does!'

But that is not my idea of love, actually.

When I phoned him, Sergei said rather nasally that it was perhaps as well I wasn't coming over on Monday because he felt as though he were coming down with flu and he wouldn't want me to get it, but it will just be a little cold at the most, and very likely a *malade imaginaire* as usual.

'What's that hammering noise in the background?'

'It is nothing – some repairs I am having done. The noise is making my head go throb-throb-throb!' he intoned sepulchrally. 'I think it will soon explode!'

'Well, that would certainly make for an interesting obituary,' I said callously and he said that his health was not a joking matter and he was a pitiful wreck of his former self.

I wore a linen-mix suit in a deep but subtle shade of dark red for the photo session, and redid my eyeliner three times as my hands were shaking so much from nerves. If I am going to be famous one day I really ought to get used to this sort of thing.

Just as I was ready, Jackie rushed in and

insisted on pinning this rather tacky crystal angel brooch (with wire halo) on to my jacket, and I don't mean one of those discreet and cute little pin ones either. She is now heavily into angels and thinks they are hovering about protecting her all the time, though I would have thought they'd got better things to do than watch Jackie make mountains of paper flowers or hand-bind books.

The brooch was huge and I hoped the pin wouldn't leave a hole in my lapel afterwards, and it certainly didn't go with the diamond heart which sparkles beautifully, but it was a kind thought in a cruel world, so I had to wait until I was in the taxi and we'd driven round the corner of the harbour before I could remove it and pop it into my handbag, since she stood waving me away on the doorstep like a proud mother. (And although she is *much* older than me, she is not quite *that* old.) And if I do have angels watching my every move, goodness knows what they thought of the ones involving Sergei, though come to think of it, goodness doesn't really come into it: he's brilliant ... So perhaps I ought to think seriously about forgiving him?

Jackie's last major craze was feng shui, and she never discards the previous one, just adds a new layer of wackiness on top, and she drives me totally crackers with all that rearranging of furniture and ornaments and sneaking into my study when she comes round for coffee, hanging wooden flutes from the ceiling, not to mention the incident with the big crystal.

She is also responsible for the hideous three-legged toad with a coin in its mouth that sits on a shelf in the hall right next to the meter, as though it had just hopped in. And though I expect it has a lot of *spring*, what puzzles me is – if it was a real one – how on earth did it *excrete*? But then, I have always been prone to these earthy thoughts and often wish that Jane Austen and the Brontës had been more forthcoming about the nitty-gritty of their daily lives.

The said frog sits there supposedly attracting money into my house, which it hasn't, and luck; so when I sent off an entry to a competition in one of those idle moments between books last year and won a year's supply of chocolate, Jackie said, 'There, that's your lucky frog's doing!'

And I said I didn't call winning a year's supply of chocolate lucky because if I ate a bar a day I would be hugely obese, spotty and possibly diabetic by the end of it, and what was fortunate about *that*? So I embarked on a giveaway spree, and I can tell you, I was the most popular house in town on Halloween for the trick-or-treaters once they realized they got three bars of chocolate each, and I'm sure some of them came back several times, only you can't tell in those masks, can you? Some of them were big enough to be *parents*, which I call plain greedy, but not as greedy as I would have been had I kept all the chocolate and pigged out on a year-long basis.

Then I got rid of temptation by handing out boxes of the stuff to the local children's ward at the hospital, which seemed a bit Lady Bountiful but went down well, and to all my friend's teenage children, especially Mel who had just started at the local uni and therefore knew lots of hungry students. It's not my fault she now has acne; I'm sure she had it long before the chocolate and hopefully that new laser treatment is going to get rid of the whole lot, only Jackie isn't that well off and the treatment is expensive, so they are doing it in instalments.

Anyway, to get back to Brown's Blooms, the photo shoot was great, and two of the other Flowers were considerably more overblown than me, and the only man among them looked like something that might sidle up the plughole and scuttle around your feet while you were in the shower and I simply can't imagine *how* he gave the impression that he had a lot more than two legs, so perhaps he's related to my good-luck frog.

Miracle phoned again to ask how the next book was going, though since she was supposed to be ditching me after *Dark, Passionate Earth* I don't know why. I said it was doing very well, and told her all about the Brown's photo shoot, and then she invited me to meet her at the Ritz for coffee in the expansive sort of way she used to do occasionally, before it finally dawned on her that I was not so much a blonde bombshell as a brunette banger.

The waiter said, 'Nice to see you again, madam,' so either he says that to everyone or he's got a good memory, because I only come here when someone else is paying, but clearly Miracle thought I was now living a secret, lush lifestyle and was impressed. I had two tall lattes while describing my day with Brown's Bookshops and all the other publicity I'd had, and she said she thought my sales would go up even more after the articles came out about being a Brown's Flower; and she was waxing quite lyrical in the old Miracle mode when suddenly she clammed up and stared at me in a horribly critical and embarrassed way hissing: 'Tina!'

Then I realized I'd inadvertently stuck the two plastic coffee stirrers through my hair like chopsticks (though I daresay I'd licked them clean first), went pink with embarrassment and quickly pulled them out. Luckily the only person who seemed to notice was this rather nice businessman sitting at the next table wearing an absolutely wonderful suit that made me want to stroke it, and he winked at me.

Sergei would not have been in the least surprised or embarrassed by my behaviour – though he *might* have adjusted the stirrers so that the round ends did not project quite like Minnie Mouse ears – because he always does *exactly* what he feels like doing, but Miracle sighed deeply and said what with having Sergei Popov as my lover and my eccentric ways, she only hoped any publicity *was* good publicity.

If she'd been regretting letting me go up to that point, I think the impulse to try and chivvy me back into the fold waned rapidly, and then she made small distressed moaning sounds when she paid the bill, though actually she always does that when obliged to part with money, and I'm sure it's much more cringe-making than anything I do.

Fourteen

Frozen Assets

Ruddles End Farm,
  Briskett

Dear Tina,
  If I may make so bold with your Christian name!
Thank you so much for your assessment of my
novel and all your good advice, which you will be
pleased to hear I am following to the letter.
  I am grateful that you got back to me so quickly
because you seem (if the papers are to be believed)
to live quite an exciting social life! I don't know
much about ballet, but Glenda says that Sergei
Popov is famous, although he is getting on a bit so
she doesn't think he dances much now, but clearly
you find fit older men attractive and she said she
will have to watch me! (Ha! Ha!)
  I have read a few Westerns now and enjoyed
them, and the only thing puzzling me is what to call
myself, because Neville Strudwick doesn't sound
right. Anyway, I just wanted to run a few ideas past
you and see what you thought: Tex Neville, Cody

Zane, or my favourite, Tex Bullwhip? Or Larry Bullwhip? Or even Bullwhip O'Sullivan?

I have now taken out all the pieces about farming that you listed, which makes the book much shorter, but the Westerns all seem to be shorter anyway. It is quite an undertaking though, and it suddenly occurred to me that my old friend George is now living only about fifty miles away from Shrimphaven, so that I could very easily come over and discuss the matter with you in person next time I visit him. Perhaps you would have dinner with me?

Since I know what you look like from the wonderful picture on the back of your books, I thought you might be curious about me, so have enclosed a recent snapshot. Everyone says I look much younger in the flesh, and nowhere near my age!

Looking forward to your reply,
Neville
(Bullwhip O'Sullivan!)

I haven't seen Sergei for two weeks – three from the last Monday I was there – because of the Brown's promotion. He insists he's suffering from terrible flu and says he does not want me to get it, so even though he is a total hypochondriac clearly he's caught something. He was definitely at home suffering because I called him several times to enquire as to his germ status.

He was quite emotional on the phone and

said I was the love of his life and he didn't deserve my forgiveness, and if anything happened to him he hoped I would always remember him with affection, and stuff like that. It was unexpectedly thoughtful of him to insist I didn't visit him in case I caught the flu too.

My heart was so softened by bathos and absence that I left a care-parcel of caviar, chocolates, flowers and champagne (which I could ill afford) on the upmarket plague victim's doorstep one day, and popped a cheery card through the letterbox before tiptoeing quietly away.

The wooden shutters were pulled across the windows, imprisoning the muslin curtains, and faint strains of music could be heard – not 'The Rite Of Spring' but something rather melancholy and indefinably Russian, as is Sergei, though you'd think he'd at least have lost all trace of an accent after all these years. Grigor sounds totally British and he hasn't been here for half as long.

Linny was fatter if anything and gloomier too, so I stayed over on Thursday night to try and cheer her up and we had dinner at the literati and glitterati-rich Lemonia. I was hoping as usual that some of the magic fairy dust of fame would rub off on my wings, but not up my nose, which is small and perfectly formed already and so does not need re-designing into a mono-snout.

We settled down to spotting the minor celebs but there was no one really *exciting* in tonight, not even someone exciting's children. Then, as we were looking at the wine list, she said suddenly that she didn't seem to fancy alcohol somehow, wasn't it funny? And she had gone totally off tea and coffee too.

'Maybe you're pregnant?' I said jokingly, though it's not funny to Tertius, actually, who would *love* children though Linny has been hot and cold about it for years, which is just as well since she's never managed to start one.

Well, she looked at me like someone had tent-pegged the idea into her head with a mallet, and I stared back at her and said, 'Linny, you're *not*, are you?'

'I simply never *thought* of that, after all this time,' she said in a peculiar voice, and just at this interesting – if faintly appalling – moment, who should walk into the Lemonia but Sergei with Tube Man on his arm. If I hadn't been sitting down, I would have fallen over.

Linny continued to stare pallidly at me, her lips silently moving, while I looked beyond her wondering if I was hallucinating. Sergei still stood near the door gesticulating vehemently – but then, he always thinks he's so famous he doesn't need to book a table, one will magically appear (and actually, he's quite right, one very often does). Then he caught my eye, smiled brilliantly, and began to make his way towards me with Tube Man following behind along with a protesting waiter, though Sergei's smile vanished when he saw Linny with me, and he's only really met her to talk to a few times and so hasn't had a chance to dislike her, so I don't know why – unless he took against her when she popped round with that message for me that time?

'Oh God, *he's* not joining us, is he?' Linny said just then, emerging from her stunned state long enough to follow the direction of my eyes and register what was happening, and I was a bit surprised since she's always fancied him, until she added distractedly: 'I can't think straight!' and went *totally* scarlet. Obviously it's nothing personal, she's just stunned by the preggie idea and only wants to make a bolt for the nearest all-night chemist, not make conversation with my some-time lover *and* a stranger.

'That's Tube Man with Sergei!' I hissed.

'Tube Man?' Linny repeated, then she looked up, her eyes widening. 'Not *the* Tube Man, Heathcliff of your novels? I thought you'd invented him!'

'No, he's real, and he's here *now* and heading this way with my lover!' I snapped. 'Pull yourself together, Linny – I need you!'

'Ah, Tsarina – Linny – you don't mind if we join you?' Sergei stated rather than asked, leaning over the table to kiss me enthusiastically and Linny rather gingerly – but that might be because Linny's facial hair was looking *particularly* rampant tonight, though probably that was just the lighting.

The waiter rearranged chairs and squeezed them in somehow, and I was immediately distracted from Tube Man's presence by the sight of Sergei's face close-up, looking bruised and sort of tight and odd under heavy make-up, more as if he'd been in a fight than had the flu and anyway I've never known him to go *out* wearing full stage slap.

Grabbing his arm, I gasped, 'Sergei, what on earth has happened to your f—?'

But he interrupted me – talked *right* over me, in fact: 'Let me introduce to you Nathan Cedar, Tsarina. Nathan, this is the friend of my heart Tina Devino, and—'

His voice went on and on in the background but I was lost to the world, gazing across the table into gorgeously treacly dark eyes ... Drowning unresisting in warm molasses ... Sinking serendipitously into...

'Tina!' Linny said sharply, and I sighed deeply and came back round in time to hear

151

Sergei lavishly ordering champagne (though he drinks it like water anyway) because he had something to celebrate. Which, knowing Sergei, could be anything from winning a Lifetime Achievement Award for his contribution to ballet, to finding the false eyelash he lost a month previously.

Tube Man (or *Nathan* as I suppose I must learn to call him now) and I were still sort of half-smiling at each other when Sergei announced: 'I have written my memoirs, Tina. Full and frank in every detail, and Nathan here is representing me – and already a publisher has taken it, and serial rights have been sold to the *Sunday Times*, so it will be a bestseller, for clearly *all* wish to know about Sergei Popov!'

Linny said hollowly that *she* knew enough already, and I said to Sergei, 'Writing your *memoirs*? But – why didn't you tell me? I thought – I mean all this last year when you have seemed so preoccupied and—'

Then I stopped dead as something else he'd said registered and turned back to Nathan: 'You are a literary agent?'

'Yes – I used to work for Bigg and Blew, but now I've set up on my own as the Cedar Literary Agency. I only intended doing fiction until Sergei persuaded me otherwise. And do you mean that you are *the* Tina Devino, the *novelist*?'

We both laughed and agreed it was a small world, especially the publishing one, and he said he must have been *stupid* not to have made the connection straight away, because he'd seen me about and he'd read all my books (which he said quite unselfconsciously so – big relieved sigh – he doesn't realize he's the frigging *hero* in them) which had my photo on the back. And I said yes, I was often in this part of London as I was an old friend of Sergei (the man currently looking jealous and sulky under his Pan-Stik foundation) and my friend Linny also lived nearby in Primrose Hill.

Linny broke in and said, 'Do you live nearby too, Nathan?'

He said he lived round the corner from Sergei, actually, and they'd first met in the deli and got talking about this bizarre incident when the fountain in the square had its basin filled with bleeding red roses, and then to my surprise Linny asked him straight out if he'd read one of her manuscripts.

There is hope for her writing yet if she can seize the opportunity like that, especially when at least half of what brain she possesses must have been wondering if pregnancy bras came in 36FF.

While he was professionally fielding that one, I turned and took a good long look at Sergei, who shifted uneasily under my scrutiny, and asked him if he'd been fighting.

'Not at all,' he said stuffily. 'I had a little fall when made dizzy by the flu and bruised my face.'

'I don't know about bruised,' I said critically, 'it looks more as if it's been stretched, pummelled and frozen.' But even as the words left my mouth, the penny dropped and I realized he hadn't had flu at all, but a facelift or something else fairly radical in the Peter Pan line.

'Oh God, Sergei, what have you *done*?' I hissed, appalled. 'I loved the character in your face, and all the wrinkles and lines! How *could* you?'

He vehemently denied having had a facelift at all. 'Perhaps just a little Botox here and there, Tsarina,' he said evasively, but I *knew*. (And so did Linny, she said later: she recognized the symptoms instantly, due to all her friends having had something done to their faces.)

'I am looking younger already,' he said complacently, recovering his sangfroid. 'Soon you will grow accustomed – now you are jealous that younger women will find me irresistible!'

And I said no *I* wouldn't and no *they* wouldn't, though actually he always has been pretty irresistible to everybody, it's just the way he is. Why did I have to go and fall for a handsome, tricky, devious, secretive man *again?* Wasn't *marrying* one enough for me?

'And that foundation you're wearing is entirely the wrong colour,' I added rather pettishly, and turned back to the infinitely more natural and Heathcliffian features of Nathan.

He was just telling Linny that he would look at her most recent book, but he could not *promise* anything, when I caught his eye and asked if he fancied having *me* as well.

He went a bit pink under his tan and said he thought I was already *with* someone, glancing at Sergei who was glowering into his champagne. And you can only sustain just so much of this innuendo in the presence of a jealous lover, so I said not at all, actually I was parting company with my present agent, Miracle Threaple, and desperately needed another. He said he knew Miracle, and if I was serious, why didn't we get together on Wednesday and talk it over? He gave me his card.

He is clearly uncertain about the situation between Sergei and me, and long may he remain so. And so am I, come to that, but I do not see why I shouldn't have my cake and eat it, because Sergei does, after all, although now I have met Tube Man I am feeling terribly ambivalent because it's like dieting:

sometimes it's enough just to *look* at the cake, you don't have to eat it and if you do you know the pleasure will be momentary and the pain horrendous.

It was all a bit tricky, and so I wasn't *that* upset when Linny dragged me away early, saying we were going on somewhere, which we were – we went on to the nearest all-night chemist by taxi.

And my God, she *is* going to have a tiny Tertius!

Fifteen

Past Notes

NOVELTINA LITERARY AND
CRITICAL AGENCY
Mudlark Cottage, The Harbour, Shrimphaven.

Dear Ms Pucklington,
  Or Elvira, as you have so kindly asked me to call you.
  I am absolutely delighted to hear of the instant acceptance of Beyond Rubber *by Red Hot Candy Press, a well-deserved success, and am deeply touched by your intention of dedicating the book to me. I certainly look forward to that signed copy you have kindly offered to send me as soon as it is in print!*
  This is surely the start of a long and happy career and I will observe your progress with interest.
  With many congratulations,
  Tina Devino

Back home in my own chaste bed by midnight due to Tertius arriving home unexpectedly to find us both swooning over the preggie test, and talk about being a gooseberry – they hardly realized I was there, what with Linny being in a deep state of shock and Tershie delirious with pleasure. So I said I *really* wanted to get back home, and didn't protest for once when Tershie sent me off in a taxi with a fistful of tenners, and really I ought to give the extra ones back because he gave me way too much.

Of course I phoned Sergei the second I got in because he does not generally go to bed before the dawn and probably not at all when he's just had darts and pintucks sewn into his face, which has *got* to hurt, and actually I could hear faint strains of music and voices chatting in the background just like most nights *chez* Popov.

'Sergei,' I said, 'in your full and frank memoirs, what did you say about me?'

He insisted that he had named no names but just said that although he had had many lovers over the years only one woman did he *truly* love with all his heart, and he had referred to me simply as 'T'.

I said people were going to guess, though, weren't they? And by the way, were these many lovers before, or concurrent with, this great love for me?

'Poof – they were nothing!' he assured me, which didn't answer anything. 'I exaggerate,

I change things a little – but mostly I write about my *brilliant* career and many, many successes...'

Then he started to enumerate his starring roles and I blanked it out as usual, just like I used to do with Tim and his eternal bloody football. But from long force of habit I broke in before he got on to the subject of the overweight ballerina who had so irrevocably strained his back while lifting her and prematurely ended his career, and asked, 'But can I read it now, Sergei, so I know what to expect?'

'No, my beloved Tina, because I wish to place the first copy of the book into your hands myself,' he said, which sounds romantic enough except that by then millions of *Sunday Times* readers, me included, will already have seen chunks of it.

Eventually I gave up. 'I'll have to go, Sergei – I'm exhausted,' I said, and I must have been, because I forgot to tell him about Linny's news – not that it has quite sunk in yet, it seems so improbable.

'Goodnight, my darling Tsarina,' he said in his terribly sexy voice, but it didn't seem to work when I knew he looked like Frankenstein's monster after a Trinny and Susannah makeover.

My mind went whipping round in circles all

night, faster than Minnie in her little wheel, while the wind howled and thundered down the chimney of my cottage as if it was on Linny's diet. Only *now* she will be able to eat anything she likes, for clearly Tertius will be absolute putty in her hands – and how *could* my oldest friend do this to me? I mean, life is never going to be the same with an infant in the offing, is it?

Not surprisingly, I couldn't sleep: if I shut my eyes I saw Tube Man's delightful dark ones smiling at me, and if I opened them I heard Sergei's voice saying he was going to publish full and frank memoirs, and worried just *how* full and frank, even if he wasn't naming names?

Certainly Tube Man – I mean *Nathan* – will have realized by now that I am the 'T' of the book, and I'd *really* like to know how much *he* knows about my private life – which seems to be becoming less and less private by the day.

But maybe all this is the price I have to pay for fame? And if Sergei's book is a bit *too* full and frank, would that be good publicity or bad? And what is Nathan thinking about me now he knows who I am? Does it matter? I mean, he may be gorgeous and haunt my dreams, but if he's going to become my agent that's *all* he must be allowed to haunt, because it just isn't going to *work* otherwise, is it? Not that I don't fancy him even more now I've actually seen him close up – and he seemed to like me, too ... only once he's remembered all the ghastly things Sergei's probably written about our so great passion he might change his mind.

I really *need* to see that manuscript!

Well, I tossed and turned all night, and come the morning I'd made my mind up that I was going to sneak into Sergei's flat and see if I could get a peek at the manuscript while he was off teaching his prancing pupils, this being his day for his Royal Ballet master-class.

I had the key ... what I couldn't think of was a good *excuse* should I be found out. I just had to hope that no one noticed me and I didn't get caught – *and* that Nathan didn't have the only copy of the memoirs.

I arrived mid-morning when I knew the coast would be clear, trying to look casual, because after all everyone locally would have seen me coming and going for years. But my heart was hammering as I tripped gaily down the steps, unlocked the door and stepped into the quiet flat – the quiet *dark* flat, for the back wall seemed to have been curtained off with thick, opaque blue polythene, presumably against builder's dust. His renovations must more extensive than I thought.

Considering how well I know the flat, it felt very odd to be standing there in the silent semi-dark – but of course I have not been there alone since Petruschka went through the great cat flap in the sky.

In fact, it was ages and ages since I'd even stayed overnight. Years. I've always preferred to sleep in my own place, to love and then be alone, as it were, and so has Sergei, fortunately, besides being a morning person like me, and actually when you think about it we are similar in more ways than you would ever dream of. Besides, if I have to stay over in London, I prefer to go to Linny's, where I can have a luxurious little en-suite to myself and come and go as I please.

Wondering if he'd turned it into an office, I stuck my head into the tiny boxroom, but it was still a rather sparsely furnished bedroom. There was a photo of Sergei with Grigor on the chest of drawers, and clothes hanging in the wardrobe that didn't look like Sergei's sort of thing at all, which was odd...

Grigor couldn't be *living* here, could he? I mean, Sergei had found it difficult enough sharing his personal space with a *cat*, let alone another ego. (Though come to think of it, cats have pretty big egos too.) Maybe Sergei simply let his protégé store some things here, or Grigor was between flats, or something?

Puzzled, I went out of the room and back to my normal habitat where my own glossy picture stared back at me from a mirrored Venetian frame surrounded by a collection of empty-eyed masks, while huge black and white arty photos of Sergei flying about through the air in every possible pose adorned all the other walls. He has thigh muscles like you wouldn't *believe*.

I found what I was searching for in the cubbyhole off the kitchen where he keeps his bureau, adrift with press cuttings and other memorabilia. There was a laptop and a wad of manuscript, inexpertly typed and entitled: *Travels Through a Life* by Sergei Popov and I'm sure that's been used before? But then, there is no copyright in titles just as there is no copyright in plots, which is just as well when half the books that come out these days seem to be either based on someone else's or Shakespeare, who is a bottomless mine of gold as far as most writers are concerned, as is Jane Austen.

But certainly no one else has lived Sergei's life, so *that* will be entirely novel, and also full marks to him for effort, because at least it looks like he has written the whole damned thing *himself* – no ghosts required.

I sat at his desk, took the elastic band off and began to flick through the pages, but there was an awful lot of it and I quickly realized there wasn't time to go through the whole thing. So instead I concentrated on trying to find 'T', whom he touchingly referred to as his 'great love' when I did track myself down, although you couldn't fail to notice that *all* the other letters of the alphabet seemed to be randomly scattered throughout as well.

I couldn't see anything *explicit* – and so far as I could tell, his full and frank disclosures seem to be more in the nature of, 'I have had many, *many* lovers in my life...' rather than a blow-by-blow account of what he got up to with them, so that is all right, I *think*. I mean, 'T' could be anyone, couldn't it? And if people draw conclusions – well, I don't have to admit it, I can still carry on with the enigmatic stuff.

I was just trying to find the more recent parts to see what he'd said about being faithful to me – or not – when the grating of a key in the front door lock turned the blood in my veins to ice.

There is something lithe and fast about the way a dancer moves on stage – and generally something languid and slow *off* it. Even so, he was there in the doorway while I was still standing clutching pages of manuscript to my frozen heart.

'Tina?'

'Grigor?'

'What are you doing here?' we exclaimed in unison.

He looked just as guilty and startled as I probably did, then his eye fell on the pages of manuscript I was still holding and he stepped into the room saying, 'I think I came on the same mission you did, Tina. I want to see just what Sergei has said about me in his memoirs.'

'What were you expecting?' I enquired coldly as he approached. I'd forgotten just how *very* tall and muscular he is close to, and my back was up against the desk with nowhere to retreat to.

'Probably not what you think,' he said thoughtfully, 'but I *do* have an interest.'

'Oh?' Turning casually, I laid the papers back on to the stack and repositioned the whole thing just the way I found it. 'Well, I only had time to flick through, so it could take you hours to find yourself. I'll leave you to it, shall I?'

He was now staring, slightly aghast, at the huge heap. 'Is it chronological? I didn't expect it to be quite *this* big, and he might come back early today. Maybe I should just wait for it to be published, only—'

'He refers to most people by nicknames or just a letter,' I said helpfully, since he was still blocking my way out. 'Shall we have a quick look at what G has been up to? Only

I've seen some of your things in the spare room while I was searching, so perhaps you'd like to enlighten *me* about what you are afraid of finding?'

He ran his fingers through his dark hair in a strangely familiar gesture, and then suddenly gave me rather a nice smile and said, 'Oh, what the hell! We may both be here for the same thing but for *entirely* different reasons, and I'm *tired* of pretending and having innuendoes made about me and Sergei all the time—'

But I knew what he was going to say before he said it: something about the smile, and the way it changed his face, and his airily expansive gestures.

'Sergei's my father,' Grigor said. 'He left me and my mother behind in Russia when he came here.'

'I'd guessed,' I told him (even though it was only by a five-second margin), then frowned. 'So, he doesn't want to acknowledge you?' It seemed surprisingly ungenerous of Sergei.

'No, I don't want him to acknowledge me!' he said fiercely. 'I didn't want to get any breaks because of who my father was. I wanted to get them because I was the *best*.'

He was terribly arrogant. 'You are *amazingly* like Sergei really,' I said. 'I'm surprised I haven't spotted it before.'

'No, I am *not* like him in the least. I am now entirely British, I don't go around like a Russian aristo in a bad old film speaking broken English, and also I am *completely* faithful to my girlfriend whom I will marry when we have saved the deposit for a house.'

'No, I see I was wrong, you're not a bit like your father, Grigor!'

'Please call me Greg – all my friends do.'

'OK. Now, do you want to look some more to see if he acknowledges you in the book?'

He shrugged: 'I suppose it doesn't matter now if he does – and perhaps he will not really want to admit to a son of my age, making him look old?'

'You're probably right about that, he's been a bit touchy lately about getting older. And now you have made it, you don't need to worry about people attributing it to his influence, do you?'

I shut the bureau lid. 'Perhaps we'd better let sleeping manuscripts lie – and Grigor, er ... Greg, I won't tell about *your* visit, if you don't tell about *mine*.'

'Right,' he said, looking relieved. 'He's forgotten he loaned me a key ages ago when I brought that stuff here to store, and I've never given it back.'

'Ditto,' I said. 'I had one so I could look after his cat and I forgot to give *mine* back, too.'

Time was getting on, and with a quick check to see we'd left no trace of our presence we tiptoed out of the silent flat and climbed the steps up to the street where Grigor shook my hand in a rather formal way and we each departed in different directions.

I felt like Tina the Spy.

The clandestine visit had been illuminating, just not in quite the way I had envisaged.

Sixteen

Fêted

NOVELTINA LITERARY AND
CRITICAL AGENCY
Mudlark Cottage, The Harbour, Shrimphaven.

Dear Neville Strudwick,
Thank you for your letter, photograph and kind invitation to dinner. However, I have made it my strict policy not to meet with my clients, since I am a professional writer with a very busy life and thus have to fit my agency work in wherever I can. I am sure you will understand.
However, I can critique your Western when you have written it (on receipt of a further cheque), and certainly do go with Bullwhip O'Sullivan. I think you are on to a real winner there.
Yours sincerely,
Tina Devino

The annual Shrimphaven Cultural Festival is looming, and Lady Het Woodwind-Chote, chairwoman of the committee running it (and the town, the county and probably the *country*) just rang to invite me for coffee, because she says she wants to ask me something *very important* regarding the festival, and I am thrilled because it must mean that now I'm famous enough to open it, not just do a book event at the library, and so I will have to write a graceful little speech – and what on earth will I wear?

I'll have to buy something new, and it's in May, which is a dodgy month weather-wise because it might be cold or hot, you never know, and not all of it is inside.

And come to that, what do I wear for coffee with Het? I mean, I know she's a friend of Jackie's, who is from an old family even if she *is* an ageing hippy with no money, but I don't move in the same social circles unless they happen to be circling one of Jackie's many bashes where anything goes, and usually does ... and where was I?

Oh yes – Het lives in a decaying pile of bricks outside town and breeds peculiar little dogs called Wiener Schnitzels or something, and I've only ever seen her in a waxed drover's coat down to her wellies looking like an escaped tarpaulin, except for the aforementioned parties and festival, when she's firmly upholstered in black with sensible court shoes and Royal Stuart tartan stockings.

I don't *do* tartan – or shiny, come to that – so unflattering.

A phone call from Linny, who had to leave the house and use her mobile, since Tershie is insisting she rests all the time and eats good food, and although she has no objection to lying about in bed eating chocolates she doesn't want to do it during valuable shopping time.

Luckily he is off on a business trip tomorrow so she can resume normal life, and perhaps he will have calmed down a bit by the time he returns.

When I asked Linny how she *felt* she said she just couldn't believe it was true, like not believing that men really had landed on the moon, because it all seemed so *unlikely*, but actually all she felt was fed up and a bit hormonal.

She wanted me to go round next day but I told her I had too much to do – which I have – but promised to pop in after seeing Sergei on Monday. 'And I sincerely hope he looks less grotesque because his face looked *terrible* the other night,' I added. 'Frozen as well as battered and bruised.'

'That's Botox,' she said knowledgeably. 'They must have overdone it, which is a pity because he normally has a very mobile face, hasn't he? It takes months to wear off – *and* he's had a facelift too, I could tell.'

'Well, I wish he hadn't. I loved him just the

way he was, and now I don't know *how* I feel, and until he looks more like his old self I'm not going to even *consider* forgiving him for the *incident* ... and I run a manuscript *assessment* service, for God's sake, so he might at least have told me he was writing his autobiography and asked me for help! Oh, and I forgot to tell you, Linny – I broke in to his flat and looked at his memoirs.'

'You did?' she gasped. *'Tina!* But did he – what did he say – you know...? Did he name *names*?'

'No, on the whole he seems to have been very cautious, and used *initials* for the women in his life. Most of the alphabet, too! But as far as I could see at least he cast them all in minor roles apart from *me*. I only had time for a quick look.'

And I didn't tell her about Grigor being Sergei's son because she is a big gossip and will never manage to keep *that* nugget to herself.

'Oh, I'm just so relieved for you,' she said kindly. 'I was worried he'd tell *all* the intimate things you wouldn't want to share with the entire world, because he has *no* natural shame whatsoever, has he?'

And I agreed that modesty and decorum were not his middle names, which actually are something unpronounceable like Ivanovitch Tolstoyevski, but hopefully Nathan

Cedar would curb any tendency to include anything *actionable* in his memoirs.

Then she said that she'd actually sneaked out to drop her manuscript off at Nathan's as arranged, though he'd just taken it from her on the doorstep because he'd had another writer with him and wasn't he gorgeous? She wasn't surprised I'd used him in my novels. She could see I'd quite like to use him *out* of them too, and Sergei had suspected the same from the way we'd been staring into each other's eyes at the Lemonia, so I'd better watch my step.

However, I do not need the warning, the minefield before me is perfectly clearly marked out already in both the Cyrillic and English alphabets.

NOVELTINA LITERARY AND CRITICAL AGENCY
Mudlark Cottage, The Harbour, Shrimphaven.

Dear Angie Heartsease,

Thank you for the manuscript together with the delightful gossamer skirt.

On first glance your novel has a rather Alice Thomas Ellis look to it, but I will give you my critique once I have had time to study it more closely.

Yes, do tell Bob Woodelf that I would be prepared to take his children's story book (written on hand-

made paper with illustrations drawn in ink distilled from toadstools), in exchange for the matching top to go with the skirt, size 12, same colour, although I do not generally deal with anything other than adult fiction.

I assume you barter among yourselves as well as with the general public to get the things you need. It seems a very practical way of going about things!

Yours sincerely,

Tina Devino

I have received a ticket for the SFWWR (Society For Women Writing Romance) Awards Lunch at the Savoy, inviting me to sit on the Salubrious Press table, which came from Tim by way of Jinni, saying it was an oversight and it should have been delivered *weeks* ago, which it certainly is because the lunch is on Friday.

And after thinking about it I have come to the conclusion that it wasn't done like this at the last minute as an *insult*, which was my first thought, but because sales of *Spring Breezes* are proving so embarrassingly good they simply can't ignore me as they intended to.

I suppose I will go ... but it's always held in one of those huge glittering dining rooms with mirrored walls and doors, and after only a couple of drinks it all gets *very* confusing, and last time I was blundering about

174

for *ages* trying to sneak out to the (very swish) ladies' cloakroom until a waiter kindly took pity on me and opened a door, though fortunately I was *far* from being the only one batting against the walls like a moth against a lantern, so the staff are used to it, and they might as well detail one of those nice young men to point out the door *permanently* at these functions and have done with it.

Just as well I already have the suit I bought for the Brown's Flowers of Fiction thing because there is no time to find anything new, and I wonder if I wore my amazing corset-style bustier under it, whether that would be too over-the-top for lunchtime in more ways than one?

I expect it was that Brown's coverage that finally caused Tim to send me the ticket, and Miracle has just called to inform me that *Spring Breezes* is currently at number twenty-two and still climbing in the Hot Chick Fiction Chart, and although I am not a chick, I *am* fiction and *hot*, so that's great.

Miracle didn't ask me to sit at her table for the lunch like she usually does (though she always expects me to pay for my own ticket), but there is a limit to the number of blonde one-hit-wonders you can accommodate at one table, and at this rate they would soon only be able to attend stand-up buffets.

Seventeen

Fresh Cuttings

NOVELTINA LITERARY AND CRITICAL AGENCY
Mudlark Cottage, The Harbour, Shrimphaven.

Dear Neville Strudwick,
Thank you for your letter.
No, I absolutely can't make any exceptions among my authors, and so will unfortunately have to decline that dinner invitation. I have heard that the Robust Langoustine at Priory Chase is very well thought of, though, so perhaps you and your friend George could enjoy that 'intimate dinner for two' instead?
I am so glad you are pressing on with your re-write, but unhappily, due to sheer pressure of work, I find I will be unable to critique the finished novel after all, which in any case might now be much better suited to a male reader. I have suggested one or two names and addresses for you to try on a separate sheet, and wish you good luck with your future writing.
Yours sincerely,
Tina Devino

Nathan does live literally round the corner from Sergei (which is probably another good reason for not attempting any kind of three-part harmony) though his flat is much smaller and his study the size of an average broom cupboard, but he does also own the cellar, and once he can afford it is going to have it converted to further living accommodation.

I elicited all this information from him within the first few minutes of arriving (surprisingly nervously) on his doorstep, also clocking his casual clothes, heart-wrenching smile and burgeoningly virile five o'clock shadow, all of which I daresay will soon be making an appearance in *The Orchid Huntress*.

While he went to make coffee I spent the time staring around the study at the piles of manuscripts, shelves of books by *terribly* well-known authors, and *especially* at the picture on his desk of a pretty girl with a vaguely familiar actressy look about her.

It's a pity people don't seem to give each other signed photos any more (except for Sergei, who hands them out to everyone – there was one propped up on a bookcase) because a scrawled 'Yours for ever, Louise' or 'From your loving sister Kate' would have been terribly helpful...

And what was I expecting anyway? That he would be living a celibate life waiting for Tina Devino to come along and make him an offer he couldn't refuse?

Then my eyes fell on a manuscript with Linny's name on it, and I quickly glanced at the top page and it was *totally* Mills and Boon, so if she's been sending her novels anywhere else she's been wasting her time and Tershie's money, though come to think of it, even posting out a hundred manuscripts would be the merest drop in the ocean of his wealth.

Fortunately I heard the clink of crockery before Nathan came back, so was sitting demurely, ankles crossed, when he came in. Over the chocolate Hobnobs I put him in the picture regarding my contractual situation with Salubrious Press, and told him how my ex, Tim, had suddenly become my editor so that they planned to release *Dark, Passionate Earth* with indecent haste in paperback and hardback at once in June, and then Miracle had given me to understand that that was *it*, they wouldn't want the option on another.

They certainly hadn't done anything to promote *Spring Breezes*, I'd done it myself – with the help of the tabloids, who'd got hold of some ridiculous story about Sergei and someone they assumed was me in his garden, and it was all quite ridiculous – but I didn't mind so long as my book sold. And actually it was wonderful now because I was getting publicity including the Brown's promotion simply for myself and *not* because I was in a relationship with a famous man, although that had never done me any harm either.

Nathan, who had listened to all this with his cup of coffee suspended in mid-air and an expression of utmost – if slightly stunned – interest, said Sergei had given him all his cuttings to look at, and since he also subscribed to the ones about me (something I *didn't* know – sweet of Sergei!), he was pretty au fait with the situation and then we started to skirt around the tricky bits, and he delicately asked, since I'd apparently been close friends with Sergei for years, how I felt about the autobiography being serialized in the national press.

Looking deeply into his treacle-brown eyes, I said I had nothing to hide, but Sergei had *assured* me that he hadn't mentioned my name in his book, or gone into specific detail, which I hoped was true. But even so it would probably all be raked up again, especially those fuzzy pictures of the woman with Sergei in the garden which they were all insinuating was me.

'So, actually it *wasn't* you in the garden?'

'Oh, *no!*' I assured him, with the limpid truthfulness engendered by lust (though had *he* had a garden larger than a window box, who knows *how* the meeting might have ended?) and then decided to follow through and, picking the woman least likely to have done any such thing, said on impulse: 'Actually, in deepest confidence, it was my old friend Linny, but it was a temporary weakness, one of those *spring* things, you know, and she deeply regrets it. She and Sergei hardly speak now, which makes it so difficult for me.' I could hardly keep my face straight, but I expect he thought the slight choking was due to emotion.

'Yes, I can see that it *would* make things difficult,' he said thoughtfully, but agreed that any publicity was great, even publicity based on unfounded rumour.

Then he said, probing carefully, 'You and Sergei are still...?'

Helpfully I assured him that my relationship with Sergei had been warm but platonic for ages (well, *hours*, really) but Sergei had a jealous nature.

He said he understood, though I'm not sure that I do, and added that he'd only intended to represent novelists, until Sergei had insisted on him handling his rights when he'd found out that he was an agent, and it was such a big coup that he couldn't resist.

And I could see he was worried that he might lose a big client if he showed more interest in me than Sergei liked ... or at least that's what I *hoped* he was worried about.

He'd already found out quite a bit about my sales figures and stuff, though don't ask me how, and thought Salubrious would now *definitely* want to take up the options clause on the next book because *Dark, Passionate Earth* seemed set to do very well, but thought we could perhaps get a better offer else-where.

I described how Miracle had so callously dropped me and that now I thought *she* was having second thoughts, too, but having been dumped I didn't want to be reconsider-ed, I wanted a new start – with *him*.

'Are you quite sure?' he said, and I said, 'Yes, I am,' and so we are agreed, and I am going to sign a contract with him.

He will have to meet with Miracle at some point to discuss my earlier books and con-tracts, but he didn't seem worried about it, so clearly there is steel in there and also, close-up, he isn't as young as I thought, probably not years and years younger than even my real age, and I wished he'd mention *who* the girl in the photo on the desk was.

But anyway, we were pronounced Agent and Author, and so went out to the pub round the corner for a celebratory lunch to celebrate our literary nuptials, which was not the sort of place either Sergei or Linny might frequent; and having got the business out of the way we found we had so much in common, like a love of plants and flowers, that we could have talked for hours except he had someone coming to see him at three and eventually had to go.

All the time we were together his lovely warm brown eyes seemed to be sending me entirely different messages to what he was saying, which is disconcerting to say the least, but I daresay I am also sending out mixed signals.

I did wear the corset-style top under my garnet red suit for the SFWWR lunch, and was glad that I did because I was photographed even though I wasn't shortlisted for the Super Romance Award – never have been, probably never will be, due to being 'light, funny and full of sexy flowers', as one of my more memorable book reviews put it.

When I jokingly asked one of the photographers to knock a few years off my age he breathed on the camera lens, so I can hardly wait to see *that* one.

Love-in-a-mist.

Tim was seated directly opposite me at the round table and I noticed he couldn't take his eyes off my diamond heart, strategically suspended just above my plunging cleavage and glittering crazily in the light from the chandeliers.

Jinni, who was sitting next to me looking like a petrified albino hamster, admired it very much, so I told her it had been given to me by a friend, and she gulped and asked if it was from Sergei Popov.

Only she'd read somewhere that we were *friends*, and she'd always loved the ballet though due to her arches she couldn't take it up professionally, and wanted to know whether he was half as gorgeous in real life as he looked on screen in that documentary about his life they did a couple of years ago. You know, the one with the memorable sequence where he danced naked in a forest, unfortunately slightly out of focus?

I was just assuring her he was twice as gorgeous in the flesh when we had to hush up and listen to the speeches, followed by some media celebrity smugly twittering on for twenty minutes, blithely informing a room mostly full of published novelists (many of whom had been earning their living writing for *years* before Ms Media had decided to cash in on her name and write her debut novel), that if we all worked *terribly* hard, and were as talented and lucky as she was, one day we might *just* manage to attain a similar glittering seat in the firmament, and become professional writers like wonderful *her* – I mean, *patronize* us, why don't you?

She was blonde, too: they're *all* blonde, but I am simply not going to let myself get a fixation about it, for I am an accredited Brunette Bloom.

After all that, and the award had been given (and I've never been sure what the significance of something that looks like a silver pomegranate on a stick is), Miracle suddenly surged up beside me shedding wonders faster than a dog sheds water, and said gushingly that I looked wonderful, and sales of *Spring Breezes* were even better, and perhaps we ought to get together again to discuss the future...

Smiling, I agreed. 'That's such a good idea, Miracle, because now I've found a new agent to take over for my next book, we *do* have a few details to sort out.'

'Oh, I *hope* you haven't done anything hasty, Tina!' she said sincerely. 'It's so hard to get a good agent, and actually I realized almost immediately that we'd been friends so long, and I have so much faith in you as a writer, that it had all been a mistake and I didn't want to lose you at all.'

So I said it was a pity she didn't tell *me* immediately if that was how she felt – or even *later* when we met at the Ritz, come to that – but actually she was quite right about a change of agent being a positive move for me, especially to someone *younger* and more go-ahead like Nathan Cedar.

'Nathan Cedar of Bigg and Blew?' she said, eyes widening.

'He was, but he's set up on his own now, and taken a few of his best writers with him – and he's also just negotiated the sale and serial rights to Sergei's autobiography and it's going to be *huge*.'

She looked totally stunned, but recovered quickly and said Nathan didn't have her contacts, to which I replied that clearly he could have *any* contacts he wanted, and I thought he'd do very well for me.

And that was that, so I have now publicly declared myself to be Nathan's property.

Then I excused myself because I could see my old editor from Salubrious waving at me over the throng, and it turned out that Ruperta is now chief fiction editor at Crimp & Letchworth! We adjourned to the American Bar for a good gossip, and I told her about changing agents, and she said now I was becoming so successful it served Miracle right for ditching me at precisely the wrong moment and why didn't we meet for lunch one day soon and talk about what I was writing now.

And so we agreed to that, and how wonderful it will be if Nathan can sell my next book to Crimp & Letchworth and I can tell Tim (politely) that I've had a better offer!

Eighteen

In Demand

NOVELTINA LITERARY AND
CRITICAL AGENCY
Mudlark Cottage, The Harbour, Shrimphaven.

Dear Wilfred Quinn,
  Thank you for your letter, cheque and most interesting manuscript.
  I haven't before received a novel entirely written in poetry. As you say, it is quite innovative – although there is nothing entirely new under the sun as far as writing goes, and didn't Vikram Seth do something like that a few years ago? Not to mention Elizabeth Barrett Browning with her Aurora Leigh.
  Yes, it was romantic that you were named after Wilfred Owen, and you are quite right not to want to change it, although I can see that editor's point: if you are writing cutting edge angry young man stuff, Wilfred doesn't somehow go, does it? However, by simply shortening it to Will Quinn you will have something that sounds just right. (And for all I

know Will Self's real name is Wilfred, so you won't be alone!)

I have enclosed my full critique on your interesting work, but I do feel that I must warn you that I think a novel of this nature would be difficult to sell to mainstream publishers, despite your brilliant record in having poetry accepted. However, the route I would suggest is that you first try to have a collection or two of poetry published in book form by a specialist poetry publisher, and then follow on this success by interesting them in your poetic novel.

I hope my advice has been of some help to you.

With best wishes for your success in your chosen field,

Tina Devino

On Monday I went to see Sergei with a heart somewhat softened by an article about him in the previous day's Sunday glossy, illustrated by a selection of *wonderful* photos of him leaping about in tights, which reminded me of how fond I am of him and the love we have shared over the years.

I was pleased to see that from a Frankenstein point of view his face looked almost back to normal, only smoothed out, as was his neck, so that the heavy make-up was absent except for a smudge of eyeliner as usual. I had been wondering where that last Gunsmoke Grey I bought went, and I am forever finding Sergei in my make-up bag.

188

I supposed I could have got used to the lack of character lines – which are bound to come back eventually, aren't they? – but the rather mask-like rigidity of his face made him seem sort of alien and cold, especially with his slanting, liquid dark eyes glistening through, so that I was less than responsive to anything other than a welcoming kiss; and in the end I had to tell him right out that it put me off, and also reminded him that I still hadn't quite forgiven him for catching him with the Blue Butterfly that time, a blow that even *diamonds* won't heal instantly, and so he would just have to resign himself to our being friends until I could come to terms with everything. Then he went profoundly sulky and accused me of wanting to ditch him for Nathan.

'You like him,' he said, crossing his arms over his chest and glaring at me. 'I could tell.'

'And *you* like Grigor,' I said coldly and un-reasonably as presumably once upon a time he'd liked Grigor's mother, which is more to the point, though of course Sergei doesn't know that I know about that yet.

And then Sergei said, 'But I do not like Grigor *that* way, as I shall show you!'

Which of course I already knew, and al-though normally I *adore* the way his English rapidly deteriorates when he is agitated, this time I fended him off because I've never felt any desire to make love to the Man In The Iron Mask, let alone the Botox one, and until the effect wears off I don't think things will ever be the same between us, and maybe not even then.

However, I am still deeply fond of Sergei despite his vanity and deviousness (or possibly *because* of them?) and we understand each other better than anyone else ever could, so although Nathan is attractive, temptation is not going to be allowed to come to anything even if he showed willing. Anyway, the complications if I ran *both* of them simultaneously would be *hideous*, and he is probably married to that skinny girl in the photo – and I'm *positive* I've seen her modelling underwear in catalogues.

No, bearing in mind my habits, not to mention *Sergei's*, Nathan is better kept as an inspirational dream – and just how bright can he *be* if he hasn't recognized himself in my books yet?

In the end, I suggested to Sergei that I would love to see some videos of his earlier starring roles which cheered him up no end. Normally you would have to fill me so full of wine I couldn't *move* before I'd sit through more than half an hour of that kind of thing, but we curled up on the sofa together while he pointed out his brilliance and I worked out the plot complications for *The Orchid Huntress.*

Watching ballet is more exhausting than sex.

Staggering round to Linny's later I found her ankle-deep in babywear catalogues, swatches of nursery wallpaper and snippets of soft furnishings, and it beats me why so many baby things have got *clowns* printed on them which I always find horrendously scary and very strange, all those weird men with red noses and white faces and stuff.

There were paint charts full of cloud pinks and bunny tail beiges, and a scattering of books with ominous sounding titles like *Get and Keep the Perfect Nanny!* which she says are all Tershie's doing, and he's already sorting out the nursery arrangements and has registered them with the best nanny agencies. She feels like a dubious starter in the motherhood stakes, especially the idea of actually giving *birth* which is so gross it doesn't bear thinking of and it's not like you can pay someone else to do it for you. So she's *not* going to think of it, she's going to have an elective caesarean under total anaesthesia and perhaps tell them to wake her up when it goes to school.

But there are compensations, because her complexion, which is normally a bit oily and sallow, is *glowing* and so is she, and there is a sort of sparkle about the eyes, and in fact the general effect is like she's fallen in love. She said much the same about *me*, only of course I have neither fallen pregnant nor fallen in love, only into sheer, crazy, inconvenient *lust* with a perfectly ordinary man ... Well, ordinary except for being extraordinarily attractive, that is.

'You're not going to ditch Sergei, are you?' Linny asked. 'I mean, you've been just like a married couple for years ... well, except for having great sex, living apart and only seeing each other one day a week. But I thought it suited you both perfectly – you seemed to have it all!'

'No, no, I couldn't imagine life without Sergei,' I agreed, for what would I do without him? Better a Botoxed ballet dancer in the bush than an agent by the hand, as the saying goes.

'Nathan dropped my manuscript off personally,' she said, 'which was kind, though he was passing anyway, and guess what? He says it is pure Mills and Boon! He suggested I make a couple of changes and then send it straight off to them, because I wouldn't need an agent.'

'No, they have standard contracts,' I agreed. 'Gosh, well done, Linny! Are you going to do what he says?'

'Oh, yes, because I simply hadn't realized I

was writing Mills and Boon, and I can see what he means now he's pointed it out, so I'm going to do exactly what he advises and then maybe *I'll* be published before too long!'

Well, I never took her seriously, but obviously I got it completely wrong! 'Did he mention me?' I asked curiously.

'No, except that he was going to be your new agent and – oh, I invited him round to dinner next Tuesday, when Tershie is home, because I've got to have lots of people back, most of them *boring*, so I thought he'd liven things up a bit! And I asked him if he had a partner he'd like to bring and he said no, so if you'd like to come and even the numbers up, you can.'

'Oh, thanks, that makes me feel *really* wanted,' I said, but actually it was a kind bit of manoeuvring on her part – or perhaps just a malicious urge to throw us together and see what happened, whichever one you wanted to think. Or maybe a bit of both?

'So he hasn't got a significant other...' I mused. 'I wonder who that girl in the photograph on his desk was then.'

Linny shrugged. 'A relative? Sister?' Then she hauled out yet another catalogue and said, 'What do you think of these hand-painted Noah's Ark storage chests? You can have the baby's name on the lid too, up to eleven letters.'

I tried to think of any name that was eleven letters long and failed dismally. 'Yes, but you couldn't have it done until after the baby was born, unless they tell you whether it is a boy or girl when you have a scan.'

'I don't want to know, I want it to be a surprise.'

'Then you'll have to choose a name that could be either sex, like ... like Hilary, Lesley or Ashley.'

'Oh, Ashley, Ashley,' she murmured, as though half-heartedly auditioning for Scarlett in *Gone With the Wind*, but I could see her mind had gone back to Bunny Tail Beige Land again.

Suddenly I felt quite left out: Linny and I had done everything together since we were eight, and now here she was setting out on one of life's major journeys without me.

When I got home I called Nathan, more for the pleasure of hearing his velvety voice than anything, and told him about Ruperta's interest in *The Orchid Huntress*, and that I was lunching with her to discuss it. He said he knew Ruperta, which caused me a twinge of jealousy, though she is married to a perfectly nice man already.

I didn't tell him I would be seeing him at Linny's next week, I thought I'd like to surprise him and see if I could tell if he was pleased or not, though actually he has very good manners so he will not be likely to look anything other than delighted, unlike Sergei, whose every passing emotion is instantly reflected on his face – or was, when he could still move it, and his rich and ever-changing landscape of expressions was one of the first things that drew me to him ... and I must just go and write that down.

NOVELTINA LITERARY AND CRITICAL AGENCY
Mudlark Cottage, The Harbour, Shrimphaven.

Dear Bob Woodelf,

Thank you for the beautiful beaded top, which I intend wearing with the matching skirt to the next Society For Women Writing Romance party at the Café Royal, always an over-the-top occasion, where I am sure it will be much admired. The wings would have been altogether too much of a good thing, so thank you for your kind offer to throw them in gratis, but I'll pass on that one.

I enclose the critique of your delightful children's tale of one boy and his elf, which had interestingly dark Tolkien and CS Lewis undertones to it. If you can increase the length by about twenty thousand words and omit the illustrations, I believe you might well sell this to a publisher, due to the sudden resurgence of that kind of thing, although I am not altogether convinced that killing the main character off at the very end (even though he is reborn as an elf) quite works for this age group.

Let me know if you want me to look at the rewritten version and recommend publishers and/or agents who might be interested. Please also tell Angie Heartsease, should she happen to flit by, that her critique will also shortly be winging its way back to her.

May Elven voices extol your *virtues too, Bob.*

Best wishes,

Tina Devino

I took the lovely top down to an elderly dressmaker in the village who is used to altering things to fit me – I am a size eight everywhere except the obvious, and so always need the shoulders and waists adjusted. I am sure it will look lovely with the skirt and feel pretty confident that no one else will be wearing the same outfit.

Once I had dropped that off I carried on up to Het's bijou mansion all geared up to gracefully accept the invitation to open the Shrimphaven Annual Festival of Culture, but it was all a great big swizz! I'd even borrowed Jackie's old stripy Puffa jacket and Hunter wellies especially, and then not only did the coffee have dog hairs floating in it from all the smelly little Wiener Schnitzels, but the Nice biscuits had been left somewhere damp for so long that they weren't.

Then Het went and pricked my smug, swollen-headed bubble (ugh, makes me sound like a big zit!) by confessing that she'd asked me round to sound me out about inviting Sergei to open the festival and be the guest of honour!

I carefully erased the disappointment out of my face while picking hairs out of my coffee, and then said I thought he *might* do it, but he didn't often visit the seaside because he thought the ozone got into his delicate sinuses and made him ill, and all that fresh salty air sapped his entire system, and she said that *was* funny, as it was the complete opposite of what most people thought.

So I explained that he usually *did* think and feel the opposite way to most people, and far from finding the seaside air bracing, he always became positively *lethargic* in Shrimp-haven.

She said, 'Oh, that doesn't sound very exciting for the festival, does it?' But I pointed out that even a lethargic Sergei was *twice* as exciting as last year's speaker, and if she was careful to give him enough champagne he'd sparkle all right.

Then she looked even more worried and said that the festival fund wouldn't run to champagne and asked whether I thought a nice fizzy perry would do instead. And I said not if they wanted him to stay longer than thirty seconds it wouldn't, though the sight of Sergei throwing a prima donna of a wobbler was always good entertainment.

Anyway, the upshot is that I am going to prepare the ground and then, unless he is absolutely against it, she will formally invite him: so we will see.

And that seemed to be that, except that as I was putting the Puffa back on, she said kindly: 'And you *will* do your usual little reading and chat in the library on the Saturday, won't you, Tina?'

I said rather tersely that I'd have to check my engagements first because I was getting booked up pretty quickly this year, and I'd get back to her, but her hide is pure rhinoceros and my pathetic little dart of importance just bounced off.

When I got home there was a mysterious message asking me to ring back, so I did, and guess what – I have been asked to do an event at *the* most prestigious three-day literary festival at Wryhove in June! Admittedly it is only because someone else has dropped out literally at the last minute, for clearly anyone who is *anyone* in the writing world is either already booked to appear or otherwise engaged and they were definitely scraping round the bottom of the rainwater butt with me.

I am to sit on a writers' panel, and also do some kind of session – I don't know *what*, or *when*, they obviously hadn't thought that far ahead yet ... and in fact, they seemed curiously relieved that I could string a sentence together on the phone. But I will prepare a reading and a short talk (perhaps about flower imagery in literature) which will be unforgettable and then they will probably invite me every year!

This is *so* exciting – at last I will be mingling on an equal footing (sort of) with the greats of the literary world.

The excitement – and nervousness – is intense ... which reminds me: I think most of the events *do* take place in tents. What on earth will I *wear*?

Nineteen

Advances

NOVELTINA LITERARY AND
CRITICAL AGENCY
Mudlark Cottage, The Harbour, Shrimphaven.

Dear Glenda Strudwick,
  Thank you for your letter, and I welcome the opportunity to assure you I have not encouraged your husband's interest in me at all, and indeed once I began to see which way the wind was blowing have done my best to put him off.
  Yes, it is distressing for you that he has turned his study into a shrine to Tina Devino – it's pretty distressing to me, too, actually – but hopefully it is just a passing phase. Yes, you are quite right – a woman in a relationship with Sergei Popov is not at all likely to be interested in your husband, and I'm not saying Neville isn't young looking and attractive for his age, but he is all yours and you are quite welcome to him.
  Now I have refused to meet him and also declined reading his rewritten novel, hopefully that will be

200

the end of the matter and his interest in me will quickly wane. If I were you, next time he goes off to visit his friend George I would make over his study as your own, with lots of frilly flowery materials and photos of fit older men on the walls. (I include one of Sergei Popov in his role as Romeo to start you off.)

With all best wishes for a resumption of your happy marriage.

Yours sincerely,
Tina Devino

Lunch with Ruperta at Garibaldi's, just like old times, and she said frankly she'd always thought I would be a *mega* success one day, due to my deeply Lawrentian symbolism and the way I managed to permeate my *entire* novels with a heady scent of sexuality without any blow by blow descriptions; not to mention roping in the readers who thought the books were about flowers, and it was about to *happen* for me, and she wanted my new book for her list at Crimp & Letchworth.

'That's fine by me, Ruperta,' I said, 'because I no longer feel a sense of loyalty to Salubrious when they were only too willing to dump me. Besides, I would love to have you as my editor again.'

Then I told her all about *The Orchid Huntress*, and said Nathan Cedar, my new agent, would send the manuscript to her as soon as he had it.

It turned out that she knew Nathan and said wasn't he *gorgeous*. Then she told me he'd nearly been married three times, but something always seemed to go wrong at the last minute and she thought it was because although he was clearly Mr Right, his ex-fiancées had all without fail run off with Mr Totally Wrong But More Exciting.

'His last fiancée was the daughter of old family friends and he'd known her for ever, so we really thought it would happen that time. I'd even bought a hat – one of those feather fascinators,' Ruperta said regretfully.

'So what went wrong?' I asked, deeply interested, as you can imagine.

'She fell for his best man. The first Nathan knew about it was a text message when they were halfway to Scotland.'

'That's quite incredible!' I said. 'And what on earth was she looking for that Nathan hadn't got?'

She shrugged. 'A bit of edge? I think perhaps Nathan is just too nice for his own good.'

I said that *nice* would be a new quality to me in an agent, since Miracle didn't do nice with any great conviction, and she said she was glad I'd changed agents because Miracle could be *very* difficult, not to mention scary.

Then Ruperta said that it was strange how getting the push from her job at Salubrious had led to wonderful new doors opening in *both* our careers. And I said yes, and the only way was up, failure was not an option. Then over tiramisu I casually mentioned that I was going to do the Wryhove Festival this year and she was deeply impressed, I could tell – and so am I actually, and I'd tell Het to stick her 'little reading session in the library' at the Shrimphaven Festival except that she thinks hers is the *only* festival in the world that matters, and anyway it would make things difficult for Jackie.

This reminded me that I hadn't sounded Sergei out about the Shrimphaven Festival yet, so when I got home I phoned him, and he was predictably not at all keen on the idea until I *swore* he wouldn't have to stand in the fresh air for any part of it (I lied), and mentioned that Lady Het Woodwind-Chote would be *personally* inviting him to open it. He is such a sucker for any form of title that he was definitely weakening so, if she plays her cards right and doesn't mention perry, she's in with a chance.

'My renovations to the back of the house are finished – you must come and see, my darling,' he said. 'It is a surprise for you.'

'I suppose you were having patio doors fitted?' I suggested, for he'd often mentioned his desire to leap straight from the house into the lush greenery of his garden in order to be at one with nature when the fancy took him, as it very often did.

'Ah-ha!' he said annoyingly. 'If I told you, it would not be a secret.'

I only hope my first guess is right, and it is not something ghastly like a Jacuzzi because sitting in a hot festering tub of breeding bacteria is not my idea of fun.

Libby Garnett is now sending me enthusiastic plans for advance publicity for the launch of *Dark, Passionate Earth*, which is a novelty, because normally I'm chasing her up by this stage, and my books don't so much get launched as dropped into a backwater and left to drift downstream as the current takes them, like discarded Pooh sticks.

But now, suddenly, *Dark, Passionate Earth* is to have a tube poster, supermarket promotion, shop-window displays in Piccadilly ... I *think* it was Piccadilly ... the works. I'll believe it all when I see it.

I am now tending to check my Amazon rankings hourly when I'm home. Should I have compulsive behaviour therapy?

The Women For Intellectual Advancement have invited me to take part in a march for peace through Shrimphaven on Sunday, and even more strangely we have all been asked to wear something sparkly and will be divided up into sections colour-wise for the march itself: doctors, teachers, housewives, intellectuals, etc, etc.

My invitation said to wear something sparkly and pink which I assumed was for all the writers until I phoned Ramona Gullet and discovered her invite said lilac, so God knows which bit they've put me into, probably at the back in Miscellaneous or Morons.

Ramona says she *never* wears lilac, it makes her look the same colour as a frog, and she doesn't possess *anything* sparkly and clearly she's not a glittery sort of person. I said the only sparkly outfit I had was a hand-beaded skirt and top which I was not going to waste on a WFIA march, and if we are both writers why do *I* have to wear girly pink?

She said God knows, and did I intend going? And I said of course not, because although of course I support peace I don't think that marching about being spangly is going to help attain it one little bit, especially somewhere like Shrimphaven where publicity will be nil – and in any case would I *want* to appear on the news as a glittery pink-clad brunette like an ethnic-nod Barbie?

Then I said I'd see her at the next Affiliated Authors meeting in London on How to Promote Yourself in the Media, and told her about the Wryhove festival, and it turns out that she will be going too, but only for the last day to do a workshop on Crime with a reading for the stronger-stomached punters.

The first of Sergei's memoir extracts has come out! But it was all about his boyhood in Russia with only occasional flashes of what is to come, to tantalize the readers into expecting something terribly revealing in the later instalments, but it's like Billy Elliot Goes Ural at the moment.

In the photo with the extract he looks terribly Slavic and beautiful and *years* younger, so either the cameraman was clever or the facelift has knocked a few years off, though come to think of it, on closer study he also looked slightly waxy and blank.

You can't say he hasn't suffered for his art, and as far as I am concerned he can carry on suffering *acute* sex deprivation too, until he can look at me while registering some appropriate emotion.

Twenty

Action Man

NOVELTINA LITERARY AND
CRITICAL AGENCY
Mudlark Cottage, The Harbour, Shrimphaven.

Dear Randi Tisward,
  Can this be your real name? I did wonder if it might be a pen name, possibly an anagram of your real one, but when I tried this all I came up with was 'isn't dirt award' which is clearly nonsense.
  Thank you for your cheque and manuscript. Yes, Newcastle-upon-Tyne does seem to be the new London of the North, doesn't it? I will get back to you with my critique as soon as I have read it.
  Yours sincerely,
  Tina Devino

I feel absolutely *devastated*! Linny just called to tell me that Nathan has asked her if he can bring someone to dinner, all terribly tactfully and he said he would understand if it was *inconvenient* so what could she say but yes.

He told Linny it was the daughter of old family friends, unexpectedly in town – and call me Sherlock Holmes, but could this be the girl he was engaged to that Ruperta told me about, who up and dumped him on the eve of their wedding? Has she come back for another bite of the cherry?

I immediately felt very possessive, but he isn't mine to possess except in an agenty sort of way, or between the covers of my books – and he must certainly never be allowed between the covers of my *bed*; so there you are, it's probably all for the best, and I made a mental note never to visit a hothouse in his company, because there is something about the verdant, steamy scent of lush greenery under glass that gets me going and I couldn't answer for the consequences.

'Are you still there?' Linny demanded. 'You've gone silent.'

'Yes, I'm still here, I was just thinking.'

'So there wasn't anything else I could do but invite her, was there? Only that makes thirteen for dinner, which won't do.'

'No it won't, but I'm not going to come, so that will make twelve now. You can tell me *everything* later in detail.'

I very nearly rang her back later and suggested I come anyway and brought Sergei with me, which would *show* everybody ... Well, I'm not sure *what* it would show, or to who, but it seemed like quite a good idea until I remembered just how Sergei behaves at private dinner parties when he actually deigns to grace them with his presence, and also that he and Linny seem to have rather taken against each other lately, so I had to give up on this idea.

Pity, I look absolutely stunning in that Titania blue beaded outfit.

The first morning of the Shrimphaven Annual Cultural Festival weekend dawned bright, breezy, and smelling of rotting fishing nets: a typical day, in fact, and had it been any other kind of day, Lady Het would have sent it back and told it to get a grip on itself.

Sergei arrived at my cottage early and dressed in beautiful suiting, looking suave and a bit exotic, what with his designer shades and glistening blue-black hair ruffled by the brisk breeze.

I'd been on the lookout for him, but all I'd seen was an early tourist with binoculars dodging about the harbour, probably looking for birds, as they do, though the only birds that hang around Shrimphaven are dreadfully common seagulls and they will find *you* at the rustle of a paper bag, there's no need to look for them.

I heard the car door slam and was in time to watch Sergei leap from the car into the cottage in three long, elastic strides, where he immediately insisted I shut all the windows, although I told him he would have to face the ozone at *some* point, since he would be standing outside the town hall opening the festival in less than an hour.

'Outside?' he said, shivering, adding pathetically that he hoped it wouldn't be the death of him, and hadn't I assured him it would all take place under cover? Then he bent and picked up something white from behind the door, though I wasn't expecting any post today since the postman only delivers on days when the wind is from the north east and magpies are flying backwards, and from the sound of it we will all soon be paying for stamps to *not* have our post delivered at all except to some pick-up point miles away, and perhaps we should all start training carrier pigeons *now*?

Sergei seemed to be engrossed by it, whatever it was.

'Is that another flyer?' I asked without much interest. 'All I seem to get these days are leaflets telling me about hearing aids and Avon catalogues, but you can have it, whatever it is.'

To my surprise he looked up at me all

slitty-eyed with suspicion. 'No, it is a letter from an admirer called Neville, saying he is here – *hot*, *ready* and *waiting*!' he snarled.

'*Neville?*' I exclaimed, startled and annoyed. 'For goodness' sake! And he's not an *admirer*, Sergei.'

'No?' Sergei said, crossing his arms over his chest and staring at me like a jack-in-the-box about to explode into action.

'Well, he sort of is,' I amended. 'I critiqued his novel and now he's got this crush on me and wants to meet me, though I've told him absolutely not.'

'So you haven't encouraged this man?'

'Of course I haven't, you imbecile,' I snapped, and added that not only had I *not* encouraged him, I'd positively *discouraged* him once I saw which way the wind was blowing, and it was all very tedious, but we would ignore it.

And then to distract him, I made Sergei his favourite kind of tea and crisp buttered toast with Gentleman's Relish, which he loves despite being no gentleman, and let him moan on and on about his allergy to ozone and his general health and the harmful effect lack of sex and sympathy from me was having on it, and how there were plenty more fish in the sea, so if I didn't love him any more, I only had to say.

And I said of course I did, and I thought

the Botox had worn off a little bit. But honestly, when he goes all whingey it gives me a real idea of what it would have been like had we married in the first flush of our love for each other, and thank God it never came to that.

As you can imagine by the time we left for the festival I was ready to enthusiastically embrace the dried-up, embittered and lonely old spinsterhood Linny's always predicting for me if I don't play my cards right.

I've left it a bit too late for Happy Families anyway: Linny may have managed to snatch the last jelly baby out of the bag, but I bet there isn't even a bit of powdered sugar at the bottom of mine.

I'd omitted to tell Sergei that, as well as opening the festival, walking around looking beautiful, and then having lunch with the Great, the Good and the Godly, he would also have to judge the Best Lobster class and crown the Lobster Princess: but perhaps he could do it long distance? It was bad enough breaking the news that he could only drive as far as the town hall car park, he'd have to walk at least two hundred yards after that in the fresh air. I didn't want to add any more bombshells and have him waltz off back to London in a huff.

When we went out I expected him to dart for the safety of his car while I locked the cottage door, but instead I heard a scuffle behind me and turned to find him hauling a thickset man with a familiar face out from behind the wall.

'Neville?' I said resignedly.

'He was staring right into the house with binoculars!' Sergei said. 'Is this the man who is annoying you, my darling, and sending the messages that insult your honour?'

Neville shook himself free of Sergei's hold, all red-faced and blustering (quite frankly he did look much better in the photograph), declaring hotly: 'Tina *wants* me to be here – she encouraged me, I could read between the lines, all right! And who could blame her if she'd rather have me than a nancy-boy dancer?'

'Now, just wait a minute...!' I began indignantly, but Sergei didn't wait – he has such a very short fuse and it was a *big* mistake calling him a nancy-boy, because although I don't think he knows the term he got the gist. He punched Neville good and hard so that he went reeling back across the road.

Sergei leapt after him like a very bouncy tiger and poor Neville turned to flee, collided with a bollard, tripped over a mooring rope, and fell headlong into the harbour with a mighty splash.

Lucky the tide was in, really, even if the flotsam is usually very dubious.

Sergei dusted himself off and pulled down his cuffs. 'There, that will be a lesson to him!' He looked terribly pleased with himself, as men do in these situations, and seemed to have entirely forgotten all about the ozone being deadly. He didn't even notice his rather battered knuckles, but said masterfully, 'Come, Tina – we had better head for the ceremony.'

'Shouldn't we see if Neville's drowned first?' I suggested.

But when I peered over the edge, he hadn't. Instead he was swimming round in circles like a mentally challenged water rat, and luckily just then one of the lifeboat men came along with a hooked thing on a stick and attempted to fish him out, so we left them to it and drove off.

Well, at least the fracas caused Sergei to be in a good mood throughout the proceedings, although the lobster judging, which took place while I was doing my well-attended library session, was apparently done long distance since he flatly refused to touch any of them.

Then he went on to astonish everyone by choosing an overdeveloped brunette teenager as Lobster Princess over the petite blonde everyone expected to win, but they clearly don't know his tastes run to the dark and busty. It certainly made *her* day when he put the crown of crossed lobster claws on her head with his own bruised hands and kissed her on both cheeks twice.

There was a slight commotion at the lunch when Sergei realized that I was seated some way below the salt and not next to him and insisted on a rearrangement, and although I would have been happier in a less prominent position, it *did* mean I got in all the photos, even if it was just in my supporting role of eye-candy, though what *kind* of candy I leave to your decision. Nut brittle?

There was no champagne, but luckily Het hadn't tried the perry either but settled for wine, so there was no explosion, just a sort of sad resigned look on Sergei's face as he sipped his perfectly good Chardonnay; but I think it's just as well since he was driving himself home later, and which imbecile ever let him pass his driving test is beyond me! (If he ever *did*?)

He left as soon as I said he could, and I gave him a warm – OK, hot – kiss, since he had been good *and* beautiful, and also my hero even if I didn't need one, and he cheered up no end.

And having every woman within eyeshot looking green does do something for me, too, there's no denying it.

There was no sign of Neville when I got

home, so hopefully that was the end of that little fixation. I hoped he was all right; he wasn't a young man and the sea is always cold here in Shrimphaven.

The harbour was thronged with tourists until the light faded, and then I had to go and pick a crop of pop cans, crisp packets and ice-cream wrappers out of my front garden.

Tomorrow I am staying in and working all day with the front curtains shut – oh, and ringing Linny to find out what happened at the dinner party!

Someone just delivered a large lobster to me, with a note from Lady Het saying it was a 'small appreciation of my pivotal role in the festival' by which I assume she means my getting Sergei to actually turn up rather than my own library talk.

The lobster had its claws secured with elastic bands and looked cross and entirely miserable – clearly its arrival on my doorstep was the culmination of a very bad day. I like lobster well enough when it arrives on a plate, preferably halved and grilled with garlic butter, but *not* when I have previously made its acquaintance.

It was going dark and everyone had gone home, so I carried the crabby crustacean down to the jetty and dropped it into the water, after snipping the elastic away. If it has any sense at all, it will give Shrimphaven a wide berth from now on.

I have penned Lady Het a polite thank-you note: it was a kind, if misguided, gesture.

Twenty-One

A Girl's Best Friend

NOVELTINA LITERARY AND
CRITICAL AGENCY
Mudlark Cottage, The Harbour, Shrimphaven.

Dear Glenda,
  Thank you for your letter warning me that Neville was on his way down, mania unabated.
  Unfortunately it came just too late and he has had an unfortunate contretemps with Sergei Popov, who had arrived at my cottage to prepare to open the Shrimphaven Annual Festival of Culture, and thus not only read the note your husband pushed through the letterbox, but caught him lurking behind the seawall with his binoculars.
  It was rash of Neville to call him a nancy boy, because although Sergei might look a trifle languid and effete, he is actually amazingly strong and athletic due to still doing hours of ballet exercises and his own special yoga routines every day, and I'm sure he took Neville totally by surprise.
  But hopefully the bruising will soon go down and

*no permanent damage to that eye has been in-
curred, and I am assured that the water in the
harbour, although cold, is not terribly polluted by
anything particularly toxic. Fortunately it was too
early for the little fracas to catch much attention,
and someone walked down from the lifeboat house
and dragged him out with one of those long hooked
things and we left them to it because we had to leave
for the town hall.*

*Sergei's hand was a little bruised, but such is the
perverse way of men that he seemed to actually
enjoy the incident, and so was inclined to be in a
happy and expansive mood for the rest of the day,
so something good came of it, and with any luck
this will be the absolute end of your husband's
interest in me and all our lives will go back to
normal!*

Yours sincerely,
Tina Devino

Linny says the girl Nathan brought to dinner
was a young, skinny blonde with big eyes
and a little pointed chin.

'Sounds just like the photograph I saw in
his study,' I said gloomily. 'Did they seem
friendly?'

'She certainly looked as though she *wanted*
to be,' Linny said. 'She was all over him like
a wet mist.'

So we think she *must* be the ex-fiancée, and
it looks like she's realized she's made a mis-

take and come to get him back, and who wouldn't?

I said, 'What about Nathan?' Linny said he looked a bit hounded, but not *too* put out, since the girl was very pretty if you liked that bug-eyed sort of look, and is some sort of model. I knew I'd seen her in catalogues, modelling the sort of bras that attempt to make something of nothing, which thank God neither Linny nor I have ever needed.

Linny said her boobs were growing ever larger and at this rate she soon wouldn't be able to stand upright without falling on to her face, and she didn't know how she was going to get through the next few months unless she stayed at home in a kaftan, because without a waist she just looked globular.

I have received an invitation to address the Mallard Rise week-long writers' course in some place vaguely northern that I've never heard of, though they say they have been running it for over thirty years. When I phoned Ramona she had heard of it but hadn't been, so I thought I might do it, especially since the speaker the following night was a novelist I particularly wanted to hear.

But when I contacted them it turned out they are offering me no fee, and only one night's accommodation and dinner, and if I want to stay longer I will have to pay for it, so I am in two minds, but maybe I will pay for one extra night. It seems a little *stingey* of them.

Now I am starting to be in demand I must try and be a bit more choosy about this kind of thing, and only do the ones where they *pay* me or the prestige is enormous, or both.

Sergei was still in masterful mode on the Monday morning, the battle scars on his fist adorned with colourful sticking plasters, and no sooner had I stepped across the threshold than he told me to close my eyes because the surprise was ready for unveiling, and I thought I could guess what it was and things might be a little tricky...

But then he led me away from the direction of the bedroom and I could feel light on my eyelids and hear a musical sort of trickling noise and when he told me to open my eyes I was standing in a tall conservatory at the back of the house, bare apart from a small spouting water feature.

'What do you think, my Tina?' he enquired anxiously. 'I did it for you – I know how you love hothouses and you can order any plants you wish, I give you free rein.'

What did I *think*? Well, my first thought

was that it was just as well it wasn't already hot, steamy and full of foliage or I might have weakened ... in fact, since my mind's eye immediately presented me with an image of what it would look like when finished and furnished, I felt distinctly softened already.

'Oh, Sergei, it will be lovely – thank you!' I said, kissing him. 'But how on earth did you get permission for such a big conservatory? Didn't the upstairs tenants object?'

'No, for I have bought the rest of the house,' he said simply. 'Did I not mention that?'

'No!'

He shrugged. 'I thought I had. It was some time ago, for the investment.'

'Well, I'm sure it was a good idea,' I said, revising my previous estimate of how much he was actually worth in an upwards direction. Then I got back to the engrossing matter of what to have in the new conservatory. 'I think we should go tropical, don't you? Warm and lush and exotic...'

A bit like Sergei himself really.

My evident delight with his surprise made him even more pleased with himself than he was when I arrived, but instead of trying to lure me into the bedroom, which I expected, he swept me off by taxi to shower me with yet more expensive diamonds in the form of earrings to match my pendant, so his book advance was clearly rather larger than mine have ever been, but, actually, it's Sergei's unpredictability that has always formed a major part of his attraction for me.

He bought himself another ring, although his hands sound like clashing cymbals already if he claps, and then we had lunch at the Café Royal, so I was glad I was looking quite smart, because you never know where you will end up with Sergei when he's in this sort of mood.

Over coffee I wrote him out a list of all the plants and palm trees and so on that I thought he should have in the conservatory and he said he had seen a wicker daybed and matching reclining chairs that would complete the look, he thought, if the cushions were recovered in the fabric of his choice (and you can just imagine the sort of thing his taste runs to – *bizarre* isn't in it). It was all great fun.

On the way back he stopped the taxi long enough to get out and buy the most enormous bouquet of roses, which was romantic even if they did unfortunately remind me of Valentine's Day. Then he held my hand and said he must have been *insane* not to have asked me to marry him before I found out his true nature, though actually we'd *both* have been insane soon after the ceremony if we'd done anything so stupid, but I *do* love him really, and he loves me and I did *know* what he was like right from the start.

We were both exhausted with shopping and emotion by the time we got back to his flat, and so retired to the baroque splendour of Sergei's bed to recuperate; and while he soon seemed fully recovered I felt even more exhausted and it was getting terribly late, and the thought of going inside my quiet little cottage and shutting the door on the world (and even Sergei) was exerting its usual magnetic pull, so I left him sitting sipping tea from a gilded green glass among his heaped-up silken pillows like a Pasha, and headed home.

Walking along the street my legs suddenly went rubbery, and the very idea of hopping on tubes and trains seemed impossible, especially with a fortune in diamonds glittering in my ears, so I decided to stop at Linny's and call a taxi.

If Tershie wasn't about I could tell her that Sergei and I had made it up, and if Tershie was about maybe he would have one of his generous impulses and offer to pay for my taxi home with his own generous, if hairy, hands.

But despite feeling as limp as a wet lettuce I was very, very happy and ... well, content, I suppose, and full of anticipation – though I expect that was simply due to the many happy hours I looked forward to spending in a specialist garden centre with carte blanche to buy what I liked.

Twenty-Two

The Butterfly Ball

It had entirely slipped my mind that Linny had told me she was going out with Tertius tonight, until I walked into the hall through the half-open front door and found her dressed as a butterfly for a fancy-dress charity ball, which was a *big* mistake in more ways than one, because pregnant butterflies are thin on the *ground* let alone in the air – and how *could* we ever have mistaken that little round bump for fat?

But Tertius in a toga was looking so adoringly at her that I swallowed any sarcastic comments, even when she put her blue-feathered Venetian butterfly mask on and headed out to the taxi that had just arrived to whisk them away and ... and...

Blue butterfly mask? Big buxom brunette? It couldn't *possibly* be, could it? *Could* it?

The Penny of Enlightenment might have taken some time to drop, but when it did it ricocheted around the echoing well of my intellect like nobody's business: Linny's concern over what Sergei had said about the other woman, her urging us to get back together ... even her relief, which I'd thought was for *me*, when I told her he'd named no lovers in his book!

Lost in my epiphany I stood on the doorstep looking after them. '*Et tu*, Linny?' I said, and her feathered face looked back at me over her shoulder in an all at once horribly memorable way ... And if this baby has pointy ears, a wicked grin and Slavic cheekbones then she is in big, big trouble with more than just Tertius.

Oh my God!

'I've called you a taxi, Tina,' Tertius said kindly, emerging from the house. 'It'll be here shortly – just pull the door closed after you when you leave, won't you?' And with a pat on my shoulder he jumped into the waiting cab and they vanished.

I was still standing there when my taxi arrived, but I did remember to turn and slam the door at the last minute – after the driver pointed it out to me.

And why do I always get a chatty taxi driver when I'm too upset to string words together and just want to be left alone? I mean, do I inflict endless boring stories about my childhood holidays by the seaside on hapless, distraught strangers? No, I do not!

The moment I got home I phoned Sergei and told him I knew all about his and Linny's affair because I'd just seen her in the blue butterfly mask, although this time mercifully *clothed*, and how could he possibly do that to me with my *best friend*?

And he said he hadn't had a relationship with anyone other than me, especially with Linny, who clearly didn't understand the artistic temperament, and I was his *only* beloved, as he'd shown me today, and he couldn't live without me.

'And so we should put the past all behind us, Tsarina, because these little incidents mean nothing to me compared to our so-great love.'

Obviously, he sees a clear distinction between our love affair and recreational sex that I can't, especially when it's with my best friend.

However, he wouldn't straight-out admit it, so I said I was going to see Linny next morning and get the truth from her if he wouldn't tell me. I put the phone down on him while he was still being persuasive in his wonderfully sexy voice.

Some die-hard little piece of me still hopes that Linny will convince me that it wasn't her, but the rest of me is shell-shocked, cold and shaking and if this is a nightmare I'd like to wake up *now*.

Early the next morning I penned a wonderful chapter of *The Orchid Huntress*, full of love, betrayal and *very* organic sex, after which I caught the train into London and burst in upon an unsuspecting Linny.

Her smile of welcome wavered when she saw my face, and then vanished completely to be replaced with one of absolute horror when I said without any preamble: 'I *know* you were the butterfly-masked lover in Sergei's flat that time. I realized it when I saw you wearing that blue mask again last night, and how *could* you? My best friend with my lover!'

She burst into a Niagara of tears and denied it between sobs rather incoherently, and told me she didn't like him anyway, and would she do that to her best friend? And I said well, would she?

Then she completely broke down and wailed, 'I only wanted to show him my Venetian mask. I'd seen his collection hanging on the wall that time I took the note round for you, and I thought he'd be interested.'

'Yes, but did you have to show him the mask in the *nude*?'

She said she wished she hadn't, it had all been a big mistake and hideously embarrassing and she was terribly sorry, and clearly it didn't mean a thing to Sergei, and I wouldn't tell Tershie, would I?

So I said what did she take me for? I, at least, was loyal to my friends – or *ex*-friends, perhaps I should say – and she'd better think up some Russian ancestry for herself in case the baby proved to be a cuckoo in the nest. Then she cried even more and said it was definitely Tershie's, she'd worked the dates out and she was sure.

And I don't know why the thought of Linny having Sergei's baby should hurt me, since I've never wanted to have a baby at all, but it did, so I said I would be going now and I never wanted to see her ever again and left her to it ... and I hope she remembers to drink something because at this rate she will be totally dehydrated and her basement will be flooded.

On the way home (by tube and train this time) I felt in a cold state of shock, especially realizing that I would never see Linny again – or not *intentionally* anyway – or have my handy base in London, or someone to tell all my secrets to, or giggle with over the clientele at the Lemonia, or discuss my love life – or lack of – with, or help her spend Tershie's money...

I mean, I've got other friends, but only one Linny.

How could she *do* this to me?

And how could Sergei do that with my best friend and think it didn't matter any more than his flings with the other passing playmates? And I know that Linny hasn't got any common sense whatsoever, but why on earth didn't Sergei think to take precautions? Or am I wrong about that, at least, and the baby is Tershie's?

Dear Tony,

Here is some news that will gladden your heart: I am no longer having any kind of relationship with Sergei Popov. All is at an end between us.

From now on I intend living a virtuous single life down here in Shrimphaven, where I will decline into a state of embittered and probably eccentric spinsterhood, so I hope you, at least, are happy.

Tina.

It being one of his days for teaching at the Royal Ballet School I rang up and had Sergei urgently summoned to the phone so I could tell him Linny had admitted everything, to which he replied dismissively that there was nothing of any importance to admit.

Then I asked him if he knew she was pregnant, and there was a short pause before he said no, but if she was it was nothing to do with him, he was careful and had learned that lesson early in life. 'Besides, Tsarina,' he added tenderly, 'you know I would never do anything that might hurt you.'

'What did you think sleeping with my best friend would do, make me *happy*?' I demanded. 'Sergei, this is the absolute *end* and I never want to see or hear from you again!'

Then I slammed the phone down, and I think I spent the entire night crying because this morning my red eyes make me look like the advance party from a Martian invasion and my throat feels husky.

I felt like half my life had suddenly been cut off, which it had actually, but it focused me on the book wonderfully well, and I threw myself into it over the next few days and didn't answer the telephone at all, just played back my messages from time to time.

There were several tearful and remorseful ones from Linny, and one from Tershie saying although he knew we'd had a little tiff, it was upsetting Linny just at a time when she shouldn't be upset, so couldn't I make it up with her? But there was no way I felt I could speak to him at the moment, or in fact anyone, I just felt too raw and betrayed.

Anyway, what sort of explanation could I possibly have given him? However awful Linny's betrayal, telling him the truth was not an option.

So I deleted all of the messages, including

the ones from Sergei, which were mostly deeply grieved, not to mention put out by my attitude and, lately, suggesting that I would be sorry when I realized to what lengths my cold heart had driven him. But I am not worried, because unless you can overdose on Russian tea he is unlikely to do his beautiful body any harm.

Then Linny started emailing me, but I just put them straight into my junk mail without opening them. There *is* no magic formula of words that can exorcise the pain of what she has done.

I only wished I could pour my heart out to Jackie, who has lots of common sense despite all her wacky ideas, but even though Linny has so totally betrayed our friendship I still couldn't do it. Jackie could see I was deeply upset about something, though, and came round do a cleansing ritual with lots of metal bowls and a bunch of smoking twigs that set the fire alarm off.

Anyway, after a few days I began to feel quite cold, calm and business-like and had a huge chunk of my book done, just the right mood for when Tim the Suit rang me in order to be *nice* in a gritted-teeth, I-have-to-do-this kind of way. He said that we seemed to have inadvertently got off on the wrong foot, but there was no reason why we couldn't get on better, just because we had a

shared history, since we were both profes-
sionals, and why didn't we get together for
lunch tomorrow if I was free and talk over
my future with Salubrious.

'I'd love to – as long as I can bring my
agent,' I said sweetly.

'That's fine by me,' he agreed, and I didn't
tell him it wasn't Miracle any more.

Fortunately when I phoned Nathan he was
free to come, and we planned to meet earlier
so we can go together. I'm *dying* to see Tim's
face when he realizes, which at least gives me
something to look forward to!

Twenty-Three

Occupied Territory

NOVELTINA LITERARY AND CRITICAL AGENCY
Mudlark Cottage, The Harbour, Shrimphaven.

Dear Randi Tisward,
  I enclose your manuscript and full critique of The Blood-Red Tyne.
  Initially the work gave me some problems, since you have written it in a stream-of-consciousness way that I have not seen since I was forced to read James Joyce in school.
  When you get past this though, there is actually a jolly good murder mystery in there, and I loved your detective, Baz Hankin, the accidental sleuth. The setting too is all very interesting, atmospheric and well done, although it can't always *be foggy even by the Tyne, can it?*
  What I think you have to do with this one, Randi, is abandon your delusion that you are writing a literary novel (which at best would only be a pale pastiche of Joyce) and concentrate on

honing up the very cutting-edge modern murder
mystery that is struggling to get out.

I have noted some indications of paragraphs and
punctuation in the margins, but perhaps you would
like to work on this aspect of it and then send it
back to me (at no further charge) so that I can
have another look at it in its new form.
Yours sincerely,
Tina Devino

Poor Tim! I felt almost sorry for him when
he looked up with a slightly tigerish smile
and spotted Nathan, and although he made
a good recovery, it really put him off his
stride.

It was very entertaining listening to him
and Nathan fencing about my future books
and contracts and stuff, and clearly Nathan
is a lot brighter than he looks despite not
having realized he's playing a starring role in
my novels, and I am perfectly willing to
prostitute my art any day, just sell me to the
highest bidder.

Tim had obviously made an effort to look
suave and sophisticated, but Nathan always
has that terribly sexy slight hint of rugged
son-of-the-soil (or maybe son-of-the-rugby-
field? I do hope not!), which is refreshing:
well it is, as long as he doesn't suddenly
reveal an all-consuming passion for some
sport.

Then Nathan and I left and went to an Affiliated Authors' meeting, which was unexciting, except for the unique feeling of turning up at a writers' event with a personable man, and Ramona was there so I introduced her, and afterwards he invited me back to his flat for coffee and a chat about things. As we were going Ramona winked at me.

When we got there Nathan said I was looking as beautiful and poised as ever, but he couldn't help noticing I was not quite my usual self and was something the matter?

And then I am afraid I got a bit tearful, though fortunately at the last minute remembering that I had already jokingly thrown Linny to the wolves; so I said I had found it difficult to forgive Linny and Sergei for what they had done together, and so I hadn't seen either of them for ages (a week *does* seem ages when you usually speak to people on the phone at least once a day, if not more, let alone *see* them), and it was all at an end between us.

All of us.

Nathan looked taken aback by this declaration, but said he understood and admired the way I was being so brave and dignified over something that must have been an awful shock. I found him very, very comforting in a cuddle-blanket kind of way, especially when he said he hated to see me cry and sat next to me on the sofa with his arm around me. And our lips were barely an inch away and closing rapidly when the door opened and we immediately sprang apart, probably looking guilty as hell, though I don't know why.

The girl from the photograph stood there, a skinny honey-blonde with startled marmoset eyes which were giving me daggers, and her pouty little mouth snapped, 'Sorry, Nathan – I didn't know you were *occupied*,' which made him sound a bit like a war zone – and come to think of it, perhaps he is, for clearly there'd be a fight if I tried to annex him. Then she turned on her four-inch stiletto heels and went out again, slamming the door. The signed photo of Sergei fell off the wall like a dire omen.

'That was Rachel,' Nathan said uncomfortably. 'She's an old friend doing some secretarial work for me until she finds a new job.'

'Right,' I said, and actually it was *fortunate* that she walked in just then and administered a cold dose of reality, because he ought not to do anything that might alienate his best paying author, Sergei, and I don't want to cause him to do that; and anyway it's always a big mistake to mix business with pleasure.

So before you knew it we were suddenly sitting far apart and talking in agent–author mode again, though our eyes were saying warmer things and clearly we share a lust that dare not speak its name.

After a while I went home with even more to think about, and just how long can I keep the threads of my life running smoothly parallel without them suddenly jumping over and knotting up? Then I remembered that I wouldn't *personally* have to worry about the Sergei thread any more, except on Nathan's account, and I went sort of cold and hollow again as though something vital had been taken away, like the last solid heart from a set of Russian matryoshka dolls.

When I was letting myself out (because Nathan was taking a phone call), Rachel came out of a door into the hall and said I must be Tina Devino, but she'd thought I was *younger*.

'And you must be Nathan's ex-fiancée,' I said pleasantly, 'but I thought you'd run off with the best man?'

And then we both smiled (lips only) and Rachel said she'd had a slight crisis with pre-wedding nerves and gone away to find herself, but Nathan *understood*, and they'd put the past behind them, and I said how lovely for her to be able to pick up where she left off and was the wedding on again? And she said all narrow-eyed that they didn't want to rush things this time and so they hadn't set a date yet. So now we know where we all are – for the moment.

Ever had the feeling you are involved in an emotional Armageddon, one that you are unlikely to win? Paradoxically, the more I get to know Nathan, the less he inspires my writing.

NOVELTINA LITERARY AND CRITICAL AGENCY
Mudlark Cottage, The Harbour, Shrimphaven.

Dear Sharon Gillespie,

Thank you for your novel, which I have read with great interest, and I believe I can now put my finger on a few of the major problems in Passing Out *that have caused you to get such a poor response from agents and editors – and full marks for perseverance, Sharon, I don't think you've missed a single one out!*

Now, in your synopsis you describe Passing Out *as a sort of historical timeslip, paranormal thriller with a love story, a bit of crime, and a slight fantasy element. But not limiting the number of genres is a huge drawback to selling your novel, because how could they market it? What on earth as?*

Regarding the timeslip element, it does not so much slip in and out of different historical ages (and, indeed, worlds) as shoot in and out like a well-greased piston – which brings me to the next major consideration: there is an awful lot of very graphically described sex, isn't there? I mean, absolutely everyone (and everything, *in chapter eight!) is at it, and almost none of it seems relevant to the plot at all. Do remember that when describing sex scenes less is* more, *because after the first few explicit (and, frankly, rather stomach-churning) descriptions, the reader does get quickly bored with it and will start flicking onwards in the hope of some kind of plot. And readers who actively prefer graphic sex scenes to plot tend to stick to books by specialist publishers such as Red Hot Candy.*

This brings me to historical accuracy. If your characters are in well-documented eras, then anachronisms like Henry V's en suite garderobe with flushing toilet stand out like a sore thumb, and will only work if you are describing a parallel universe where such oddities are perfectly acceptable.

I have gone into all these points in much greater detail in my critique, but you certainly have a fertile imagination and great sticking-power, Sharon, and those are both strong assets in a novelist!

Best wishes for your success,
Tina Devino

Twenty-Four

Dished

Having caught up with my manuscript assessments, I only had to pop them back into the post with their critiques, and then next day I set off for my speaking engagement at the Mallard Rise Writers' Week.

I hadn't told anyone other than Mel the mouse-sitter where I was because, frankly, it would be good to leave all my recent traumas behind for a couple of days even if I had to take my freshly rebroken heart with me together with the diamond one.

But I was looking forward to hearing Hereward Brunswick give his talk on Research from Life tomorrow, because hopefully it would be the uncensored bits and so very entertaining.

I caught an early train so as to get there with plenty of time to unpack and find my way about before I had to perform, and I went First Class because although you still have to listen to a lot of boring business men bleating down the phone telling their secretaries they are *on the train*, like it's going to be a big, big surprise, you do get a better class of accent doing it, plus endless cups of coffee – which was just as well, because I discovered later that Mallard Rise coffee tastes like it was made from ground-up owl pellets and possibly was.

I got off the train somewhere industrial, and then was whisked by taxi through quite promising countryside until we suddenly turned off into a seedy village, then on up a long drive to what looked like some kind of institution ... Which, sure enough, proved to be my destination, though most of it was very modern, so it was unfortunate that my room was a vast and sparsely furnished attic chamber in the one old building, spooky even in the middle of the day.

Stephen King would have felt quite at home there.

Moira, the desiccated but sprightly pensioner deputized to show me the ropes, seemed to think she deserved congratulations that I was not sharing the attic with anyone else, since the many small bunk-bedded compartments leading off it were often used for the overflow of late-bookers. (And serve them jolly well right, too, her tone implied.)

After explaining that she would meet me

later to escort me to dinner where I was to dine in state with the committee, and then afterwards show me to the Great Hall to give my talk, she added that she was sure everyone would be there, even if, like her, they hadn't actually *heard* of me before, and wasn't it wonderful about Hereward Brunswick coming tomorrow? They could all hardly wait, but now she would have to leave me to settle in because she had to dash off and take her class in Successful Steps to Getting Your First Novel Published.

'Oh, I hadn't realized you were a fellow novelist,' I said. 'What do you write?'

'Religious poetry, actually. Well, see you later!'

All this gave me a feeling in my waters, as Linny so repulsively used to say ... only I am not going to think about Linny. At all. Ever again. *Or* Sergei.

I unpacked, showered in a bathroom straight out of *Psycho*, and put on the garnet suit, since no one here would have seen it, and it is certainly earning its keep, which is just as well because it was *very* expensive. And it was either wear the diamonds or carry them because my door seemed to have a very odd lock on it. You could only lock it from the outside so when you were inside you couldn't tell if it was locked or not.

The place just got weirder and weirder.

So I wore my glitzy baubles thinking they might be over the top but at least they'd be *unforgettable*, which meant I would be too, and from what I've heard about him Hereward Brunswick was unlikely to be big in the *bling* department so there wouldn't be a lot of competition.

Then, just as I was gilding the lily with a bit of blusher, this sort of factory foghorn blasted out right under my window, and suddenly the lawn outside was full of scurrying octogenarians heading, presumably, for the dining room. I hurried down the three flights of stairs, where Moira collected me impatiently and rushed me into a big bare room full of long tables, a bit Dickensian apart from all the Formica.

'You've missed the bar, I'm afraid, if you drink *alcohol*,' she said blithely. 'It opens for ten minutes before dinner to allow members to buy wine or have a pre-dinner drink, but I am a teetotaller, as are Deirdre and Felicity here.'

I exchanged stiff smiles with two more Moira clones, then she quickly introduced me to the other members of the committee, whose names I decided to forget instantly, and call all the women Moira and the men Ted, which served them right for their tendency to call *me* Nina.

I took my place as directed in the only

empty chair at the end of the table, and then they said we might as well begin, and would I like to do the honours?

The honours? Of course! So I joined my hands and said quickly: 'For what we are about to receive, may the Lord God make us truly thankful,' which showed a trusting faith, as it turned out.

One of the Moiras said, 'Thank you, dear: and now perhaps you'd like to dish out?'

'Dish out?' I echoed, then realized that all the serving dishes and the stack of plates were lined up right in front of me, and was informed that the person in the catbird seat always served, and they took it in turns.

Clearly it was all a cunning plot. Had I known I was doling out the slop like a dinner lady I wouldn't have worn my best suit, that's for sure, besides all this not being quite how I had expected to be treated as tonight's guest of honour and speaker.

Anyway, I stood up and took the lid off the biggest dish, and there was this huge, glistening white mound like the Quatermass experiment gone wrong, and one of the Teds exclaimed: 'Oh, goody, mashed potatoes!'

Then I took the lids off the other two and there were sausages – *one* each – and pallid life-leached vegetables that looked as though they'd been cooked for a month.

Oh, yummy!

It actually tasted even worse than it sounds, and the texture of the bits that *didn't* taste of anything at all was indescribable, and I'm not sure what the dessert was because, having dished it out, I wasn't feeling inclined to experiment with my health any further. Then the full glory of the coffee burst upon me and it all began to seem like some hellish nightmare, but then, so does my entire life lately.

It seemed even more ghastly when I was marched, biliously, to the Great Hall, a minor aeroplane hangar with dodgy acoustics, where the chairman stood at the microphone telling bad jokes for ages before he let me anywhere near it.

When I finally had the talking stick, though, I went into automatic and whipped through my usual 'who I am, what I write, and funny anecdotes' spiel in a spirit of 'let's get it over with', because after that it was going to be more a case of 'I'm an author – get me out of here!'

My talk was followed by lots of questions from the audience of the 'I've been writing for thirty years, how do I get my first novel accepted?' kind, to which there is no easy answer ... or even *any* answer, except that there is always *hope*.

Then the chairman thanked me, adding that the bar was now open, and I was astonished that no one got trampled to death in the rush. Certainly by the time I got there the queue was a mile deep, due to my having been detained and interrogated by the committee just like the Spanish inquisition but without the fun factor; *and* by Moira, who gave me the list of next day's events so I could join in, though frankly I think I'm *beyond* Plotting for Beginners, or Self-publishing the Easy Way. But Post-mortem Procedure for Crime Writers sounded interesting if you had a strong stomach and might prepare me to face dinner with more stoicism.

I gave up on the bar and I'd had enough of the committee, so I retired to my haunted chamber where I spent most of the night with the light on and the TV murmuring for company, while people I couldn't see trod the creaking floorboards.

I had just managed to drop off with the dawn when I was jolted out of bed by that damned klaxon again.

Breakfast hit a whole new low, even though I hadn't thought food *could* get worse than last night's dinner, and calling custard scrambled egg fools nobody even if you do dollop it on a piece of limp toast first. And although there were six whole fresh grapefruit on a side table you had to queue for them, *and* the one sharp knife to cut and segment them with, otherwise it was Blunt Teaspoons at Dawn, and so I gave up and I'm surprised the ones there for a whole week don't get beriberi.

I did try and drink the coffee, but by the time breakfast was over I was starting to get acute caffeine withdrawal symptoms, so once everyone had rushed off to their group sessions I phoned for a taxi and begged the driver to take me to the nearest decent cup of coffee, which proved to be at a pottery factory and showroom with a tea shop attached, a few miles away.

I told him to collect me in a couple of hours, and I've done half my Christmas shopping already even if it will be a bit heavy to get home on the train, and the coffee was wonderful and came in soup bowls, so it will just have to keep me going until I get back on the train tomorrow. I also bought a supply of pastries and nuts and things to take back with me so I don't have to eat dinner tonight; I can just pretend.

You can't say I don't learn from experience, and I was at the front of the queue for the bar's brief opening, and got a whole bottle of wine despite the barman's horror at the idea.

'I'm sure you only mean a large *glass*, not a whole bottle, dear?' he said kindly, but I insisted and carried it off to the dining room where I made sure I wasn't at the dodgy dishing-out end of the table this time and pretended not to hear when the committee arrived and Moira said I was sitting in *her* chair.

Then Hereward Brunswick turned up, escorted by another Moira clone, and of course *he* drew the short straw this time, and it is amazing that they can treat even a famous author like that! Or try to, because Hereward said flat out that he was positive they would understand that he'd rather sit next to me because he was such a great admirer of my books, and he was *sure* Deirdre wouldn't mind changing with him?

She couldn't do much except agree, and Hereward is a very entertaining, but very *naughty* old boy and told me some stories about Miracle (who is his agent) that I hadn't heard; but of course he's been with her from way back, even before she set up her own agency.

We shared the rest of my bottle of wine after he'd given his rather risqué but fun talk to the assembled Teds and Moiras, then we retired to a quiet corner of the bar and spent the evening together – but not in any amorous way on *my* part, I hasten to add.

But I did buy his latest book, *The Nelson Incident*, and he signed it '*To that rare sexy flower, Tina Devino, from her would-bee pollinator!*' He is absolutely wicked, but actually he's still very dishy even now, so you can imagine what he would have been like twenty years ago – he'd have given Sergei a run for his money.

At the end of the evening he was collected by a big black car and departed waving regally, since he lives somewhere within ferrying distance, and I wished I did. (And don't think he didn't pressingly invite me to go back with him, either – but of course I tactfully declined.)

I was certainly glad to get back home next day, all laden with books and pottery as I was, though fortunately a very nice man helped me off the train and into a taxi with them, so it was not as difficult as I envisaged.

The answering machine was crammed full of tearful, hurt and/or indignant messages from Sergei and Linny which I quickly deleted.

Minnie wore the smug expression of a mouse who'd been spoilt rotten in my absence and her furry little belly was so full she was practically dragging it along the cage floor.

'Get on that treadmill and run!' I told her, but she just gave me a look of disdain and twitched her whiskers a bit.

Twenty-Five

Watering Places

Dear Tony,

I was deeply touched by your brotherly offer to go and duff Sergei up personally for breaking your sister's heart.

However, my heart isn't broken, just a bit bruised, so I would much rather you didn't attempt any such thing.

Do thank Mary for the delicious home-baked cake, made to that recipe given to you by our cousin umpteen times removed, Tullia, the one you unearthed on your fact-finding mission to Italy in search of the ancestors. I'm glad something constructive came out of the trip.

Your affectionate sister,
Tina.

Next day my author copies of both the paperback and hardback of *Dark, Passionate Earth* arrived, and rather splendid they looked, too; it was nice to have them before they actually came out in the shops, which is what used to happen.

Oh, and did I tell you I'm having an *actual* book launch tomorrow at a bar opposite Salubrious House? No? Well, it was all a *complete* surprise to me, so it just shows that advance orders must be good.

Nathan is going to be there too and except for the break-up I might have asked Sergei … only then he would probably have over-shadowed me because of his fame and whopping great charisma, plus his other striking personal attributes – and frankly I don't want to *share* the limelight at all, this is *my* moment! But I would have asked Linny to go with me under other circumstances – like her not having slept with my lover, for instance.

I wore something lighter and sassier than a suit this time, which is just as well because the wine bar was crammed full and very hot, but then this sort of thing usually is because all the publishing staff dash in for free booze and nibbles, and then just as quickly pour out again, leaving only the hard core of people who have to be there.

Tim had to be pleasant to me, and Nathan said I looked *beautiful* and the book was going to be a *big* success, and he stayed next to me practically the whole time, even though Jinni did her best to lure him away, and full marks to her for effort. God knows I don't blame her because the publishing world is *full* of women, which is why when you see even an old Suit at these affairs they are always entirely *surrounded* by attractive women, charmed by the novelty, and even Tim seemed to have no trouble attracting several, despite the lack of hair and dyspeptic expression.

I loved the balloons with trowels and things printed on them that they'd decked the room with, though the ribbed green cucumber ones looked a bit like inflated condoms ... and when I had a closer look I could have sworn...

But no, *surely* not? And the big, helium rose-shaped ones were very tasteful, so I took one home with me.

Several people mentioned the latest extract from Sergei's memoirs, especially hinting about the mysterious 'T', love of his life, and asking how I felt about the papers linking me with those photos of Sergei and a naked woman in his garden. Oh, and hadn't Sergei and I been friends for years?

But I was back to the enigmatic smile and the bland: 'Do they *really*?' because clearly I can make it on my own, I don't need any two-timing Bolsheviks to boost *my* ratings.

Dark, Passionate Earth seems to be everywhere, and so am I, signing it – and this time sometimes I actually *sit* and sign it for *people*, though if anyone else implies anything about me and Sergei I'm going to lob a copy at their heads and I fear the enigmatic smile may soon turn into a snarl.

And I kept remembering the lower-key book tour with *Spring Breezes* when Linny and I had such fun despite the awful weather and the Repetitive Signing Syndrome, and the bookshop manager in Harrods *remembered* Linny and asked after her, so I lied and said she was abroad on holiday.

Still, I was cheered to see my book emblazoned all over the tube – must ask for a copy of the poster to brighten my hovel – not to mention all the other publicity and reviews it was getting, and so I embarked on my second day of book signings feeling quite confident. There was even a little queue at the first one except that it turned out that half of them thought I was the war correspondent who was signing next day. Don't they ever read the *information*?

But I seemed to have mastered the technique of looking up and smiling without actually *looking* at who was buying the book while asking: 'And who shall I make it out to?' in an interested way, until suddenly this little waterlogged voice said: 'To your lowly worm of a friend Linny, who doesn't deserve *ever* to be forgiven, but who misses you!'

It was, too, and she looked *dreadful,* all pale and miserable, and I sprang up and we gave each other a big hug and my eyes went all watery, which was not exactly the image I was trying to project. It was just as well Linny now looks so *preggie* because otherwise the people queuing might have thought we were a pair of *lesbians,* though on second thoughts I daresay that doesn't matter these days and might even be a promotional plus, and in any case with my name linked so luridly with Sergei's on everyone's lips there isn't much chance of *that.*

'Oh, Linny, I've missed you too!' I cried.

And she said, 'Tina, life just isn't the same without you! I can't say exactly what I think to anyone else, even Tershie, and I *hate* being pregnant – I feel like something out of *Alien,* wondering what's going to pop out, and I must have been absolutely *mad* ... and I don't know what got into me!'

I said Sergei had that effect on a lot of women, and though I could never forgive him, I understood just why she'd done it, and although it was always going to feel odd that we'd – however temporarily – shared a lover, our friendship was worth more than that.

Then we hugged again and the manager brought another chair over and suggested my friend sit down and wait while I finished my signing, which she did, and then came in the taxi with me to the last one.

Afterwards we went on to the Ritz where she bought us both a celebratory afternoon tea once we'd tidied our rather ravaged faces in the swish ladies' loo. (And the waiter said it was nice to see me again, madam, so I nearly asked whether they wanted a writer in residence or even just anything expensive promoted in my next book.)

We settled down over the teacups to a major, major catch-up of everything that's been happening to us both, and hers sounds much worse, and they should warn you what pregnancy's *like*, it all sounds *appalling*, and no wonder the birth rate is falling.

Then we went back to Linny's, where Tershie also embraced me, smelling of some fabulously expensive aftershave, and said he was glad we'd made up our spat (little does he know the cause and he's never going to learn it from me). He phoned the Lemonia to see if they could find us a table and they could, so we had *another* celebration and I felt like I'd done nothing but sign books, eat and drink all day, and could there be a more perfect way to spend your time?

Tershie sent me home in a taxi again, only unfortunately it turned out to be the driver who spent the last long journey telling me about his seaside holidays as a child, and it wasn't any more interesting the second time round than the first.

I feel like I've had a lifeline restored now that I'm speaking to Linny again – and she's just rung to say that her Mills and Boon has been accepted! Subject to a *major* rewrite, of course, but Linny – accepted! She says Tershie is terribly proud of her, and now she feels that she can call herself a writer at last instead of being secretly envious of my success, even though she was always delighted for me.

I said I'd only just had any success, and I was sure she'd be a *mega* seller, so now she is coming to the SFWWR Summer Party with me, where she will meet lots of other M&B writers, which will be useful, without feeling that she's just tagging along.

Nathan, too, has now fallen into the habit of phoning me up (although sometimes at rather strange hours of the day or night) for little chats about nothing much, which is lovely, and we get on *so* well, and he sort of fills the place Sergei used to occupy with his daily phone calls telling me how his feet hurt, or how he had a mysterious ache somewhere, though I still just don't know what to do with myself on Mondays.

I wore my Titania blue beaded outfit for the SFWWR party, and Linny wore something slightly tented in beige, which is *not* a colour that goes well with her rather Mediterranean complexion, but I didn't like to tell her, and actually when I took off the retro blue and pink-spotted chiffon scarf I was wearing, which I didn't really *need* with all that bead action, and tucked it into her neckline, it brightened the whole thing up no end.

I drank too much, talked too much, but didn't *eat* too much, since Linny had to get a passing waiter in an armlock before he'd stop wafting past with trays of finger food held tantalizingly high above our heads and we only had time to grab a handful before he struggled free. He gave us a wide berth after that, but these places are all the same when it comes to the catering at functions, and so *uninspired* when it comes to nibbles that I can't help feeling it would be much better if they just sent someone down to Marks and Spencer's with a trolley.

My book is climbing briskly up the paperback charts *and* doing brilliantly on Amazon, and I seem to be *everywhere* ... not to mention having the next somewhat steamy bit of Sergei's memoirs come out (I must have missed that part when I was looking through the manuscript!), where he had gone into our relationship and habits in a lot more depth...

So now there is a bit of scandal among the tabloids again, only neither of us is married so it's not exactly *illegal* is it? (Although, come to think of it, I think having sex in your garden may well now be against the law, and what a lot of spoilsports if so!)

And it is quite *wrong* to say Sergei 'seduced newly wed Tina Devino from the arms of her husband, Tim Hollins' because I realized ten minutes after the wedding that I'd made a major, major error, and so if anything I used Sergei as an excuse to get out of it, and who wouldn't?

Now Mel has asked me if she can start a web fan club! She says she loves my books, which I knew, and she thought she could make some money out of it since everyone would have to pay to join and then she could flog them Tina Devino official souvenirs and so on ... and Minnie the mouse is going to be the official mascot with a big photo – the Melinda Moussenger of the web world.

Dark, Passionate Earth is now number two in the paperback charts!

Am I famous yet?

Twenty-Six

Mixed Signals

NOVELTINA LITERARY AND CRITICAL AGENCY
Mudlark Cottage, The Harbour, Shrimphaven.

Dear Glenda Strudwick,
  How nice to hear from you that everything is going so well, and that Neville made a good recovery from that nasty chill and the tummy bug, which, as you say, were probably entirely due to his unfortunate dip in the harbour and served him right.
  No, it doesn't really surprise me that he took a sudden aversion to the study, once he saw the framed photograph of Sergei and the new Laura Ashley wallpaper and curtains, but it does indeed now sound the perfect place to construct those delightful dried flower arrangements you make for the church bazaars and the Women's Institute; and yes, there probably is a good local market for greeting cards and bookmarks made from hand-pressed flowers, and you should certainly try it.

I'm sorry Neville is now underfoot in the rest of the house, although I expect you are enjoying his attempts to ingratiate himself back into your good graces, but actually I meant it when I told him he could write Westerns, so how about buying him a nice shed to work in out of the way and encouraging him to get on with it? Some of them are like little offices, and if you have it well away from the house you will hardly know he is there.

With many thanks for the super wicker cornucopia of dried summer flowers – I am sure it will be a great inspiration to me while I am working.

Best wishes,
Tina Devino

This literary life is terribly exhausting! I've been on three radio programmes (though they were all recorded at the same place!) and one morning TV thing which was *terrifying*, and I was sure I'd made a complete fool of myself, but actually when I watched the video Linny had recorded for me, I wasn't too bad! And I still can't remember a *thing* about it due to terror, but obviously under severe stress a part of my brain I didn't even realize I *had* takes over, and so I sound almost *intelligent*, which proves I have even more hidden talents than I thought.

Despite all this media coverage I still managed to fit in a signing session at Necromancer's Nook in Shrimphaven yesterday, since they've always been very good to me, and even if I'm getting quite successful there is no way I am going to get too big for my boots, because after all it's still only *me* in here, when you come right down to it, and actually lots of people came including Ramona, and Linny – and Nathan, which was a surprise, although of course I let him know my publicity itinerary.

Afterwards I invited him back for tea at the cottage – Ramona and Linny too, of course. But Ramona had to dash because if she left her dog in the car for too long it ate the upholstery, and Linny had to rush back to town in order to get ready for something – but don't worry, it's not *birth*, that's months away – so it was just the two of us.

I showed him round my garden first, which doesn't take long, six pebbles and a bit of samphire by a driftwood log, and even Sergei wouldn't dare to get up to anything in there because you would *certainly* be arrested. Then I gave him a quick guided tour of the cottage, not lingering in my tiny bedroom, because Earth girls *aren't* easy, and though it may have begun to seem like a *decade* since I last had sex with anyone I don't wish to appear at all *needy*, besides the strange dichotomy of Nathan being rather come-on-ish on the phone, but much more reserved in the flesh, apart from the expression in his warm, dark brown eyes...

And really I am starting to find all these mixed signals rather confusing so clearly I am out of practice.

We had tea in my little sitting room and fortunately I had large quantities of scones, clotted cream and strawberry jam in, ready for Mel (who I am convinced has a tapeworm, since she is stick thin except for a little round pot belly, but who eats voraciously) because she's coming round later to show me my fan club website, HotBeds. I knew she wouldn't mind sacrificing some of them in a good cause...

But perhaps *he* is too good and *I* am too wary, for although we were *very* friendly (and it's difficult to be anything else on a sofa the size of a large armchair), we weren't *that* friendly, especially when he somehow got on to the subject of cricket over the tea and scones, which seemed to be a Pavlovian trigger to happy reminiscences.

Why do men always have an engrossing interest in something boring? You try and tap their depths only to find there aren't any, just throwbacks to the playground involving balls of one kind or another...

And why do so many women pretend they share that interest? But not me: I told him straight out that I found all sport a bafflingly strange way of going on, and would rather not *think* about it, let alone *talk* about it, so he changed the subject to Sergei, with whom he seems, disconcertingly, to be getting quite friendly.

Sergei's started calling in to see him once or twice a week, and Nathan says he looks *deeply* gloomy, and I said, 'Well, he's a Russian, what do you expect?'

I mean, have you ever read any of their novels? If they aren't deeply melancholy they don't seem to have *any* plot, they're just aimed at depressing you, although *War and Peace* is a bit different and if you miss out the war it's quite a quick, fun read ... and where was I? Oh, yes – so then Nathan said no, Sergei hadn't always been like that, and he used to have a bit of joie de vivre about him, and I refrained from saying that I used to know all about that.

Sergei asked Nathan if he'd seen me lately, and if so how was I doing, and wanted to be remembered to me as if I was about to forget about him, which, short of sudden Alzheimer's, is *highly* unlikely, and even then probably my last coherent image, hanging in the air like the Cheshire cat's grin, would be of Sergei in mid-leap.

Apparently on Sergei's last visit he'd fallen into a mood of nostalgia, and said I was the most beautiful woman in the world, small but perfectly formed like a dryad. And he would *always* love me passionately, but he was afraid he had been discarded for another.

Nathan had assured him that, as far as he knew, there *was* no other man in my life – and of course *his* relationship with me was purely a businesslike one of author and agent, and Sergei then said that Nathan was his *good* friend and embraced him.

Well, I thought about that for a minute, and really, Nathan has his head screwed on the right way, even if he is a sucker for the type of women who are going to dump him for something more exciting at the first opportunity!

Nathan said that Rachel had come in last time Sergei had visited and been introduced, and Sergei had told her she would be quite pretty if she had a bit more meat on her bones, slender yet curvaceous like his beloved Tina, and she should eat more butter and cream, advice that went down like a lead balloon from the sound of it; and even while we were having our little *tête-à-tête* with the scones, Runaway Rachel rang his mobile twice, probably to check out who or what he was doing.

Nathan was kind to her in an exasperated way, so if he doesn't watch it he *will* end up married to her after all (if she doesn't take off with the vicar mid-ceremony), because he's too nice to turn her down.

He asked me if I missed Sergei as much as he seemed to miss me, and his eyes briefly rested on the photos turned to face the wall like naughty schoolchildren, though draping them in deepest mourning-black underwear *might* have been more descriptive of my feelings.

'While I will always treasure the recollection of our time together,' I said sadly (*and the diamonds, though of course I didn't mention those*), 'Sergei totally betrayed my trust.'

'But you and Linny are friends again, it seems?'

'That's quite a different kettle of fish,' I told him, and he said, 'Oh?'

But clearly there is *no* point in explaining the nuances of the situation to him because not only is he a *man*, and therefore doesn't understand the language, but how can he understand it when even I don't?

And then I added that Sergei and I had been *friends* for ages, nothing more, and he can't have been missing me that much since he certainly hadn't made a push to gain my forgiveness, apart from a few phone calls, so whatever was making him melancholy it certainly wasn't our split. Perhaps it's a side effect of Botox?

Nathan gave me one of those disconcerting looks from his treacle-coloured eyes and said if it had been him, he wouldn't have looked at any other woman in the first place, but if he had been so mad as to do so, would by now have been begging me on his knees to forgive him.

Then he suddenly jumped up and got a book from his briefcase (I was starting to wonder if he took it everywhere with him, like a security blanket) and said he had been entrusted with a gift from Sergei, then handed me an advance copy of *Travels Through a Life* – and a big, glossy tome it turned out to be, with what looked like wads of photos, which will be *entirely* of Sergei, you can bet on it.

But before I had time to open it, Mel turned up and she seemed to totally unnerve him, even though practically everyone under thirty has bright green hair in clumps and rings through everything, so he hastily thanked me for the tea, kissed me circumspectly on the cheek, gazed deeply into my eyes again, and left...

I sighed and said, 'Is he sexy, or what?'

Mel said he wasn't bad, even if he was pretty geriatric.

'*Geriatric?* He's only in his thirties!'

'Precisely,' she said and picking up Sergei's book, she began to flick through it with her pointy green fingernails.

I took it off her and got her to show me my fan site instead, which was quite exciting, and there have been lots of what she calls 'hits' already, so it might augment her student loan a bit, but I did decline the offer of a prototype *Dark, Passionate Earth* T-shirt, since that seemed a bit too much like self-advertising, even for me.

When I was alone I finally looked at Sergei's book, and not only has he signed it personally at the front with a huge flourishing, *To Tina, my only love, from her devoted Sergei*, there was an equally effusive dedication to me printed on the very next page which *no one* could miss, and it certainly blew any cover I might have had left, since even a moron would be in no doubt just who the 'T' in the book was after that.

I sat staring at the dedication until the light faded and I couldn't see it any more, thinking about my life and the empty part left by Linny's absence, now so happily refilled, and the other echoing void occupied for so long by Sergei that he was part of me, with all his strange little ways – and God knows I have enough of my own – but if either of us ever need an idiosyncrasy donor we would be a near-perfect match. I don't think I could *ever* find anyone else who would suit me like he did, even though Nathan *is* the stuff that lust is made of, and somehow I don't think that would ever be enough.

But when it comes down to it, if Sergei had *really* wanted me back, he would have done something melodramatic by now, so clearly he doesn't and this fulsome declaration in print is either a hangover from when he *did* feel that way, or a thank you and goodbye to all that, and maybe he's already found someone younger and more nubile?

I usually give him a personally signed copy of *my* latest book, so I wrote a little formal note of thanks for the dedication, signed my name in a copy of *Dark, Passionate Earth*, and packed the whole thing up to post.

That seemed to be the end of that.

I wonder if I *could* wrest Nathan away from Rachel, train him to my once-a-week no-staying-over ways, and *still* maintain (a) total secrecy from Sergei so it doesn't affect his and Nathan's author/client relationship, and (b) my own author/client relationship with Nathan as well as a more personal one?

If I solve that, maybe I could start on world peace next?

I've always wanted to be a successful novelist more than anything in the world, so now that it is almost within my grasp, why don't I feel happier?

The Willows,
Drover Road,
Up Wrigley

Dear Ms Devino,
I am sending you my latest novel, Pixies of Pilgarrow, *a delightful and traditional story of magic and enchantment in the style of Elizabeth Goudge. It is aimed at all age groups, from young adult upwards.*
I have written sixteen novels so far but have met with a total lack of response from publishers who only seem interested in smut and violence. I am certain that there is a vast market of young people out there crying out for something more inspirational! My Guide troop are all enthralled when I read my wholesome work to them as a treat when we are winding down from our more strenuous activities.
Everyone who has read any of my work has said it is unforgettable and has had an indescribable effect on them. None of my friends can understand why I wasn't published long ago!
Perhaps you can tell me where to go from here? I am getting so disheartened I am seriously thinking of taking a desktop publishing course and going it alone as the Potter-Rubrick Press!
Do advise me.
Yours sincerely,
Pippa Potter-Rubrick (Miss)

Twenty-Seven

Overtures

MEMORIZE THE FOLLOWING
ADDRESS AND THEN DESTROY!
*'Limpet', C/O Ben's News & Sweet Shop, High
Street, Brittling-by-the-Sea.*

Dear Ms Devino,
*My sources tell me you are able to operate in
complete confidentiality. This is hush-hush: you will
receive the money separately, in cash by hand, so be
prepared!*
*My novel is based on my wartime experiences,
and since I am still bound by the Official Secrets
Act, my name must never be mentioned in
connection with it. Limpet will be my pen name.
Peruse it privately – it is for your eyes only. Do not
divulge any of my details to anyone. I will not be
available for publicity when the book is published.*
Limpet

What a difference a few hours can make!
A strange postman (stranger than my usual

one, I mean) rang my bell at the crack of dawn in order to hand me a thick bundle of letters wadded together with elastic bands under a plastic wrapper, and a small register-ed padded envelope.

Naturally I opened the package first and found inside a box marked with the name of a very famous jeweller containing one small but perfect pearl. It was pierced for stringing and lay there looking very cultured: urbane, almost.

Nothing else.

Well, this profoundly puzzled me, but I put it to one side and reached for the bundle, which had been forwarded from some super post-sorting place. When I took the wrapper off there were dozens of letters from Sergei, with dates going right back to our split and, at a quick glance, running the full gamut of hurt from despair to anger, due to getting no answer whatsoever, apart from having the phone put down on him a few times.

It is *amazingly* clever of the post office to track me down eventually because, due to Sergei's habit of writing half his letters back to front and turning all his Ss into Ws, the address was illegible even to me.

I made a cup of coffee and then settled down to read my way through them in date order, although as evidenced by the addres-ses, his handwriting is hard to understand,

273

but I certainly got the gist – especially the last one saying he was going to send me a pearl a day as a symbol of his tears until I forgave him!

All was now explained, and it was the sort of lavish thing he *would* do, too, though actually I rather think he's shot himself in the foot with this one, since even if I do ever forgive him I am not going to say so until I have enough pearls for a decent sized string, am I?

But naturally I felt much happier knowing how Sergei felt about me, and clearly he was missing me ... so I could at least phone him and thank him for the pearl, couldn't I?

I did, and he seemed absolutely *overcome* to hear my voice, even though I was not ready yet to talk about forgiveness, but had rung merely to say that I had only just received his letters due to their having gone astray.

He clearly has been watching the progress of *Dark, Passionate Earth* because he knew how well it was selling.

I asked him how he was, and he said as well as sinking into a deep decline so that he was the despair of his friends, he had this strange pain in his arm, with tingling, and did I think he was going to have a heart attack? And he told me all about the trouble with his feet, and how he thought the poison from the Botox had got into his system and was slowly killing him, so if I ever brought myself to forgive him he could safely promise never to have that done again.

Other women were as nothing compared to me, he said, and without his Tsarina Tina his life was empty and meaningless, and he would never even look at anyone again if I took him back.

I said not to press me yet because he had hurt me *very* deeply and wounds like that took a long time to heal. (But to keep sending the pearls.)

NOVELTINA LITERARY AND CRITICAL AGENCY
Mudlark Cottage, The Harbour, Shrimphaven.

Dear Limpet,

Thank you for your letter and manuscript, and the money that was pushed into my shopping basket in used five-pound notes on Saturday while I was in Waitrose. You will be pleased to know that I didn't spot the person who did it, and indeed, did not even notice the envelope of money until the girl at the checkout tried to scan it.

I enclose my full critique, but I am afraid that as it stands your work is more a fictionalization of your wartime experiences than a novel. So even under a pen name it is probably still actionable under the Official Secrets Act. However, it is all a long time ago now, so perhaps if you get in touch with the appropriate authorities they might agree to an edited autobiography in due course? After all, none of it seems to particularly merit secrecy at this stage, although I am not at all trying to belittle the very, very important role you clearly paid in winning the war.

I hope this is all helpful to you. By the way, in view of your desire for absolute secrecy, perhaps I should point out to you that you have inadvertently printed your real name and address in full at the top of every sheet of the manuscript.

Yours sincerely,
Tina Devino

Sergei is back to phoning me up for frequent little chats, just as he used to do, mostly to give me an update on his health, but sometimes also to talk about his book's progress towards publication in July, and to ask me what I thought about the book itself, which of course I had read instantly.

Well, there is no doubt in my mind that it will sell like hot cakes for the photos of Sergei alone, and the narrative certainly hots up as you get towards where I come on the scene, especially that bit in the tropical greenhouse, which I had forgotten about – and there is something terribly primordial and sexy about the smell of hot, damp, steamy plants, isn't there? But clearly any shreds of cover I might have had have been blown.

Nathan's still continuing his chatty calls, too – sometimes at strange times of the day or night, sounding oddly furtive (I *must* remember to tell him I found his expensive gold fountain pen down the back of my sofa) – but although I enjoy talking to him he is *definitely* more flirtatious when he's not within reach, so I can't figure him out at all.

Also, now I have got to *know* him, I simply can't use him as a model for my sexy hero in *The Orchid Huntress* any more, because he is quite ordinary really, whereas my male protagonists always have a bit of extra something. In fact, a *lot* of extra something.

I definitely need a new hero.

Linny rang and I was just going to tell her all about the lost letters and talking to Sergei on the phone again when she blurted, fast, 'Tina, I've just done something that was really, really hard, but that I hope will help you and Sergei to heal your rift.'

'Oh God, what have you done now?' I said ungratefully.

Linny said she'd just had a meeting with Sergei at a local coffee shop (from the sound of it, both were wearing dark glasses and raincoats and looking suspicious), during which interesting conversation they had agreed that the whole butterfly incident never happened at all, or even if it did it had nothing to do with *them*, it was two other people entirely, and therefore none of us need take any notice of it, and we could all meet together in a friendly fashion as before.

This had a certain mad logic to it, and Linny certainly surprised me with *that* one, but I pointed out that it wouldn't be easy, would it, pretending we all *imagined* it?

She said Sergei had found it perfectly reasonable, and actually when she met him *she* found it quite easy too; clearly it wasn't *her* who had done those things, so now it was just me who would have to rearrange my memories a bit and then we would be all right, wouldn't we?

'Yes, I suppose we would, but what about the baby?'

'I'm not entirely stupid, you know,' she said. 'I'm positive it's Tershie's.'

Let's hope she's right.

After that I brought her up to date on Sergei's letters going astray, and the daily supply of small but perfect pearls, which she thought very, very romantic, as I suppose it is, and she thought I should forgive him because clearly we were made for each other.

'Only don't do it yet, because you can't do much with only a few small pearls.'

'I couldn't agree more,' I said. 'And Nathan's still ringing me. How come he is so warm and flirty on the phone, but all businesslike when we meet, except for the odd, small lapse, and then he retreats back instantly into agent mode? What do you make of that?'

'Maybe he's a tease?' she suggested. 'Or he fancies you like mad, only he's a bit scared of you too, so he backs off when he's actually with you?'

'Linny, pregnancy has addled your brain. How can he be scared of harmless little *moi*?'

As I expected, she couldn't think of a good answer to that one.

I've promised to spend the weekend with her, helping with the final polishing of her rewritten Mills and Boon novel, because she's not quite sure if it's how they want it. She's also a bit worried about Tershie, because he's in Colombia on business, but he's promised not to leave the hotel even for the airport without an armed guard, since Linny was frightened that he would get kidnapped, which apparently *everybody* is all the time over there, and he was dropping hints about bringing her Colombian emerald earrings.

Twenty-Eight

Pearls Among Women

NOVELTINA LITERARY AND CRITICAL AGENCY
Mudlark Cottage, The Harbour, Shrimphaven.

Dear Pippa Potter-Rubrick,
   Thank you for your letter, cheque and manu-script.
   I too was fascinated by Pixies of Pilgarrow, *and while I am not saying that it isn't somewhat in the general style of Elizabeth Goudge, it does have a certain slightly evangelical Christian tone that I don't remember her novels having.*
   Unfortunately, I don't think this type of novel is sufficiently mainstream to sell to a publisher, who would not perceive it as having a wide enough market to make it worth their while. However, were you to self-publish your books, I could imagine them doing quite well in Christian bookshops all over the place, although you would, of course, have to spend time promoting them yourself.
   Should you indeed decide to set up Potter-

Rubrick Press, I can put you in touch with another author, Bob Woodelf, who is writing not dissimilar work and who has not, so far as I am aware, managed to sell his children's novel yet. He does delightful, if uncommercial, illustrations, too.

I hope you find my critique helpful, though it is mostly confined to pointing out those places where charming whimsy tilts in the direction of twee, always a hard balance to maintain in a book of this kind. You also have a slight tendency to change from first person to third, sometimes in the same sentence, which can be disconcerting, and these I have also marked.

I wish you all the best with your inspiring work.
Yours sincerely,
Tina Devino

We actually had a fun weekend, sorting out the manuscript and shopping (even if Linny had a tendency to linger in Baby Gap), and chilling out with large quantities of fattening foods and a box of tissues in front of romantic DVDs.

Then on the Monday morning I woke up early with that feeling of anticipation I always used to get, knowing I would see Sergei soon...

Only, of course, I wasn't.

But I was too restless to go back to sleep, and then I had an idea: I would get up and walk around to Nathan's on the pretext of dropping off the pen he left behind (which I *was* actually going to push through his letter-box on my way to the station later anyway, and he wouldn't know which train I meant to get, would he?), I'd catch him early and maybe off-guard, so that he would have to ask me in for coffee at least ... and who knows what might happen then?

Well, it *seemed* like a good idea at the time.

I left a note for Linny saying I was popping out but I'd be back soon to pick up my bag, then I set out through the bright early-morning streets, glad I wasn't having to scurry off to some office for the day – even though I would soon have to scurry off to my own office in Shrimphaven and get on with *The Orchid Huntress*.

Excitement lent wings to my feet and I was soon ringing Nathan's doorbell ... but it was immediately evident that that was the *only* bell of his I was likely to ring, since the door was opened by Runaway Rachel, dressed in an insecurely tied man's bathrobe over nothing and bearing that give-away heavy-eyed look.

'Oh, it's *you*!' she said, looking taken aback, but probably not as much as I felt, although hopefully I didn't show it.

'I didn't expect to find you here this early, Rachel,' I said pleasantly, which was quite an effort, I can tell you.

She said with a smirk, 'Oh, didn't Nathan tell you I'd moved back in?'

'No, I thought it must be dress-down Friday and I'd got the wrong day of the week.'

She frowned and twitched the edges of the robe closed. 'Nathan's showering. Can I take a message?'

'Not really, I've just brought his rather swish fountain pen back. I found it down the back of the sofa and I was going to push it through the letterbox, only it looks valuable ... and anyway, people get attached to these things, don't they?'

'Yes, and he adores it, because it was a present from *me*, actually.' Then she smirked a bit more and said she was glad I'd called because I could be the first to *congratulate* them, and flashed the rock on her ring finger at me.

'Oh, is the engagement on again?' I said casually. 'That's very understanding of Nathan.'

And she said yes, he knew it had all just been pre-wedding nerves before, and I said that was *one* way of describing it, but congratulations anyway.

Then Nathan's voice called down the stairs: 'Who is it, Rachel?'

I said quickly, 'I'll let you get back to it, then. I'm just on my way to see Sergei.'

She stared at me. 'But everyone said you

and Sergei had split up!'

'Everyone is wrong then, aren't they? Just like everyone saying you and Nathan had split up, but these days hearts can be so seamlessly mended you'd never even know where the join was ... and will you excuse me, because I need to go and write that last sentence down.'

I left her on the doorstep, and I'd dug out a pen and notebook from my bag and made a note of it for *The Orchid Huntress* before I heard the door close. She could have caught her death of cold ... with a little luck.

Then I walked on round the corner and suddenly everything sort of hit me and I felt totally humiliated as though I'd been caught trying to prostitute myself, and clearly Nathan would rather have a skinny young girl than me and he was just keeping this gullible old author sweet.

I wandered on without noticing where, but my feet automatically took me right to Sergei's door, though I didn't realize it until I found myself nose to nose with a brass knocker shaped like a pair of ballet shoes, with no recollection of getting there. I was just about to turn away when it swung open to reveal Sergei, with his glowing, slightly manic dark eyes and dishevelled black hair.

'At last! At last you have forgiven me, my Tina – my *darling*!' he exclaimed in a voice broken with emotion, then swept me into a rib-crackingly muscular embrace.

After that it was hard enough to concentrate on breathing let alone *thinking*, and perhaps thinking is something I do too much of anyway and should give up?

Much later I rang Linny and told her where I was, and she said, 'What about the pearls?'

Straight to the point as usual. 'Sergei was going to take them and have them made into a necklace for me anyway, for my birthday. And we've been talking—'

She giggled, 'Well, that's one word for it!'

I continued, with dignity: 'We've been *talking*, and Sergei wants to show the world how much he loves me, so we are getting engaged.'

She shrieked, 'Engaged! You're getting *married*? Are you mad?'

'No, of course we aren't getting *married*, there's no way we could live together as man and wife! We are just getting engaged, that's all.'

She said she could see where I was coming from because it was *terribly* trendy to get engaged and it needn't *lead* to anything, and were we going to have a party?

'I hadn't thought that far ahead, but perhaps we could book the Lemonia, what do you think?'

She thought it sounded fun so I said I'd put it to Sergei. 'And do you know, he bought every single plant, tree and shrub for the conservatory on that list of suggestions I gave him, which must have cost him a fortune, because they are all tropical and some of them are very rare! Isn't that romantic?' But I didn't tell her what we did in there earlier, on the wicker daybed under its canopy of greenery.

'Yes, I suppose it is,' she agreed kindly, for she does not share my passion for plants.

Then I told her I was accompanying him to his book launch in July, so she would have to help me choose something extra special to wear for it, and just then Sergei came back into the room and that was the end of all conversation for quite some time.

Later I let Sergei drive me home himself (stopping at Linny's briefly for my case on the way), which is something I don't usually do, due to him driving like the possessed, but I was so tired I could hardly move, even to get out of the car. I even let him carry me over the threshold, which he did without one single murmur about his bad back.

Then he kissed me passionately and left with a little box of pearls in his pocket, singing something stirring in Russian.

Due to excessive languor I didn't actually do

anything constructive until next morning, when I checked my voicemail and discovered a rather incoherent and shame-faced message from Nathan, more or less saying that Rachel had foisted herself on him and put his ring back on her finger herself. He certainly hadn't done it, and he didn't want to marry her despite being still fond of her, but she was making it very difficult to say so.

But really, that is not *my* problem, so when he added, 'Rachel says you and Sergei are together again, but I don't know if that's true? I'm sure you were determined not to see him ever again, weren't you? So it seemed unlikely...' and rambled on and on again about his own problems. I deleted him.

I think I liked him better as a distant inspiration than as a *man*, and while writing the next bit of *The Orchid Huntress* I found my thoughts turning more and more to Grigor, who seems to possess most of the attributes needed in a hero, except for a slight lack in the chin department, although when I was face to face with him in Sergei's flat I realized that it is not so much that he hasn't *got* one, just that it is small and rather pointed and perhaps does not show to best advantage from a distant stage.

NOVELTINA LITERARY AND CRITICAL AGENCY
Mudlark Cottage, The Harbour, Shrimphaven.

Dear Glenda Strudwick,

Thank you for your letter.

While I am delighted to hear that Neville has had good feedback from Rangerider Books Ltd, when I encouraged him to write Westerns I certainly didn't imagine for one moment that he would then embrace the whole cowboy lifestyle, let alone insisting on being called Bullwhip O'Sullivan and wearing a Stetson all the time, which must be deeply embarrassing for you!

I do sympathize, and I can only think that he must be going through a sort of late male crisis of some kind, especially those strange ideas he was having about you dressing up in a gunbelt and cowboy hat too ... Well, quite frankly, Glenda, I would only go down that route if the idea does something for you, otherwise I'd tell him to go live in his little log cabin until he's regained his senses.

No, I didn't realize that the farm actually belonged to you – and perhaps you ought to give a timely reminder about that to your husband? You never know who he might meet at the Western Re-enactment Society, after all, though at least you can always cut your losses, as you say – if I read your reference to 'culling the old bull' correctly.

How practical you farming folk are!

With admiration and best wishes, Tina Devino

Twenty-Nine

Cross Currents

Dear Tony,
Here is some news that will, I hope, gladden your heart: Sergei and I are not only together again, but are also engaged to be married.
But don't immediately jump to conclusions and start organizing a wedding or anything, because that is the only step I am prepared to take towards respectability. Everyone is getting engaged these days as a way of signifying the permanence and depth of their love for one another – it's terribly trendy.
There will be full colour coverage of our engagement party in a magazine too, always helpful to my career, which is actually the only reason I am telling you about plighting my troth, so you don't get too overexcited when you read about it.
Your affectionate sister,
Tina

Sergei threw himself into organizing our big, fat Greek engagement party with passion, and although we'd only booked half the Lemonia all the rest of the customers were soon sucked into the festivities too, for while there may be no such thing as a free lunch, wherever Sergei is the champagne runs like water, and I sincerely hope both his book advance and his investments are still flourishing.

We'd invited an eclectic mix of people between us: there were ballet dancers (including Grigor), choreographers, ordinary friends, literary contacts, a journalist or two, a photographer, his editor, my old (and now new) editor Ruperta, and Tim (how could I resist inviting him?), who came with his colleague Jinni in tow.

Of course Tershie and Linny were there, and Jackie and Mel, plus a sprinkling of writer friends, a ballet critic, a couple of Cossacks (Sergei said he didn't remember inviting them, and anyway they were ejected halfway through the evening for being drunk and trying to dance on the tables), and Nathan with Rachel clinging possessively to his arm looking smug, an expression that turned to envy when Sergei gave a short speech paying me compliments of the effusive, blush-making kind and then presented me with a most beautiful ring.

Thank goodness he has such good taste in these things, because I will have to wear it all the time like my other decent jewellery, due to the lack of security in my cottage, and at this rate I will be decked out like a Christmas tree everywhere I go.

At least the pearl string is still a work in progress.

Every time I looked up during the evening I caught Nathan staring rather intensely at me, Rachel looking suspiciously from one to the other of us as if we might be making secret signals, and Jinni gazing adoringly at Nathan, so clearly Rachel would be better employed in watching her back than me.

There were no members of either family present, apart from the unacknowledged Grigor, since Sergei hasn't got any and the Devino contingent were thankfully still in Wales ... or so I thought until I looked up to find my brother Tony had suddenly appeared and was standing looking belligerently at Sergei.

So then of course I had to introduce them, and Tony announced loudly that he'd come to give the family blessing on my engagement, and to Sergei he said that for the honour of the family he had to agree to the wedding, and it was right that Sergei make an honest woman of me.

I could see he was really throwing himself into the role and enjoying it, though the fractured Italian accent was a bit thick at times. 'Since the untimely death of our parents, I have been as a father to her,' he said brokenly, which he hasn't, just a bossy older brother who always thought he knew best and was dying to see me married to someone respectable. Sergei does not quite seem to fit that bill, but he'd obviously despaired of my tying the knot with anyone else.

Sergei, deeply moved, sprang up, kissed him on both cheeks and said he respected his viewpoint entirely and Tony could be sure his sister was in safe hands. (And it is quite true that he has never dropped me yet.)

'We are to be brothers – let us drink to that!' he said warmly, and pressed a glass into Tony's not unwilling hand. Then they had a conversation that sounded like *War and Peace* crossed with *The Sopranos*, while the rest of the guests, the excitement over, began to take their leave.

Grigor kissed me enthusiastically as he left; a pleasure somewhat spoiled by the realization that I was only one rung below the level of being his stepmother, which was very odd to contemplate: only of course it won't actually come to that.

Eventually it was just me, Sergei and Tony.

'I'll drive Tina home to Shrimphaven,' Tony declared with a challenging look at

Sergei, though actually I was going to splash out on a taxi home anyway: I'd had enough of people for one night, even people I love. And if poor Tony thought he was removing me from temptation he was closing the stable door so long after the horse had bolted that it wasn't even a dust cloud on the horizon.

So I kissed Sergei a loving goodbye and Tony and I headed off to my cottage, where he spent a hideously uncomfortable night on my little sofa, but it *was* all his idea to take me home anyway.

He creaked off back to Wales at the crack of dawn, leaving me a message of complaint in the kitchen, including his opinion that pet mice in the house were unhygienic, though in my view not as unhygienic as dumping used tea bags in the sink and scattering toast crumbs everywhere, but I expect he was just peeved because Minnie kept him awake all night running round in her wheel. Mary obviously has a lot to put up with.

Husbands: you can't live with them – but you *can* live without them.

NOVELTINA LITERARY AND
CRITICAL AGENCY
Mudlark Cottage, The Harbour, Shrimphaven.

Dear Fanny Gotobed,
Thank you for your letter, cheque and the manuscript of your novel, One Village, One Heart.

No, I'm sure I can't imagine why those agents who asked to see your manuscript on receipt of your letter of enquiry expected something much more risqué, unless perhaps they thought your rather unusual name was a pseudonym indicative of your style?

I am so sorry to hear how recently you were widowed, and what a difficult financial situation you now find yourself in, and I truly applaud your bravery in trying to pick up the reins of the writing career you abandoned over fifty years ago. One piece of good news on this score: the charge for reading your manuscript quoted on my flyer is actually a misprint, and I am therefore sending you a cheque to refund half of it. I really must speak to my printer!

Unfortunately, the market for novels has changed slightly over the ensuing years, and apart from the perennial Miss Read I can't think of another author in print who is writing your kind of sweet, gentle village-affairs sort of book. This is not to say that people don't want to read them any more, just that publishers don't think they want to.

I certainly found One Village, One Heart

absolutely charming, but I do think you will find it
difficult to get a publisher to take it. However, all is
not lost: the novel is extremely episodic and would
lend itself brilliantly to being divided up into lots of
short stories for those magazines catering for the
older reader, for whom your work is perfect (list
appended), and who pay quite well. I think they
would love them, and who knows – once you have
had a large number accepted a publisher might just
think twice about refusing your next book!

I am quite sure you will be successful, and look
forward to reading your stories soon in magazines.

By the way, as soon as you can manage it I would
at least upgrade to an electric typewriter. It will
make your work much easier to read and so vastly
increase the chances of having it accepted.

Good luck with your writing.

Yours sincerely,
Tina Devino

Much coverage of the party in the press with
everyone looking half-cut, especially the
roped-in Lemonia clients, and no one *told*
me that that famous actor was there! (Not
that I've *seen* him in anything, but I have
heard of him.)

All the press coverage called me 'bestselling novelist Tina Devino', which was
gratifying, and most also mentioned my new,
beautiful, clingy, smoky-purple, hand-beaded and embroidered dress, which I refused

to tell anyone the source of, even Linny, because I want to keep the fairies at the bottom of my garden to myself.

My book is now firmly lodged at the top of the bestseller charts and everyone wants a piece of me – or me *and* Sergei, since the 'engaged and living miles apart' angle seems to be a strange concept to everyone, even though creative people *marrying* and living apart has been done already by several couples, I seem to recall, and worked very well. And anyway, it's our own business, although the party made us more in the public domain, I suppose, and there is now such a feeding frenzy over Sergei's memoirs that it won't surprise me if they shoot up the non-fiction bestseller charts as soon as they are out, so we may be occupying the tops of adjacent charts ... And it may surprise the readers to find that actually, despite a tendency to hyperbole when describing his own performance, Sergei writes quite well.

He was pleased with the photos in which he says he looks very young and fit, and I also look beautiful, and he is buying a new cuttings book each since both of ours are now full. He has been approached about doing a new edition of his SergeiYoga exercise DVD and book.

Ruperta has now been shown the first

chapters of *The Orchid Huntress* and has made an offer for it, as has Tim the Suit at Salubrious for rather more than my last one with them, but not enough to tempt me and so I have signed with Ruperta.

Nathan keeps looking at me with a sort of sad resignation whenever we meet, but the thought of his cut from the advance should have cheered his heart, and if he's sad because he didn't make his move before I got engaged, tough; and if it's because he doesn't want to marry Rachel any more, tough again, he should *do* something about it.

Flushed with success and money I had a tiny safe installed in my cottage and a burglar alarm, though whether they are a good idea I don't know, because when alarms go off no one ever takes any notice, so it's just a beacon screaming that there's no one there, burglars welcome, isn't it? Still, at least now it should be reasonably safe to leave some of my bits of jewellery at home, rather than carry my spoils of war around with me all the time.

Otherwise, life has resumed its normal even tenor, except that sometimes Sergei and I accept invitations to things and go out *together* as an official couple, and when I took him to an SFWWR meeting it took mc *ages* to extricate him afterwards. I nearly gave up and left him there, surrounded – and no one ever presses free copies of their steamy novels into *my* hands.

I have even been to the *ballet* with Sergei a couple of times to see Grigor leaping about! It's quite conducive to plotting out the last chapters of *The Orchid Huntress*, and I am able to totally blank out Sergei's running commentary on the finer points of the dancers' technique through long practice, while smiling faintly and nodding, back in enigmatic mode.

NOVELTINA LITERARY AND CRITICAL AGENCY
Mudlark Cottage, The Harbour, Shrimphaven.

Dear Will Quinn,

Thank you so much for the latest copy of Strimp! *containing your exciting new poem cycle 'Snort, snort, snort'. Avant-garde poetry magazines do not often come my way.*

I am so pleased that you found my advice helpful, and clearly your technique of ceaselessly *bombarding every poetry publication with your work has paid off in an increasing number of acceptances, although I am sure that would not be the case were you not such an interesting poet.*

Things are looking promising for you, and good luck with that competition with the prize of having your first poetry collection published in book form!

I will keep my fingers crossed on that one.

Meanwhile, I wouldn't give up your job just yet, unless you are an exceptional performance poet willing to go the rounds of small venues and literary festivals. Besides, your work clearly gives you lots of deeply meaningful life experience, which always makes for good copy.

I wish you every success with your writing.

Best wishes,
Tina Devino

Thirty

On Film

Dear Tony,
  I asked Sergei, and he said Russian Orthodox, whatever that is. Does this mean that you are going to forbid the banns? (Not that we intend putting them up in the first place.) Oh, do, please do!
  Tell Mary, regarding her kind enquiry as to the respective merits of bread-making machines over juicers as gifts, that I don't have a wedding list, and will never have a wedding list, because there isn't going to be a wedding. I know you are both finding this concept hard to grasp, but do try.
  Your affectionate sister,
  Tina

The Wryhove Literary Festival was looming. Now I have been fêted a bit I don't feel quite so overwhelmed by the honour, though I am aware that earning huge amounts of money has never given other non-literary authors any street credibility with the highbrow set.

  Tershie agreed to Linny coming with me

provided we booked in somewhere civilized for the duration, although at four months-ish pregnant I don't think she is particularly delicate, only Tershie is touchingly concerned about her. As it turned out, it was just as well, because apparently things get booked up for miles around absolutely months ahead, but by flourishing indecently huge amounts of money Tershie managed to install us in a swish suite in a country-house hotel fairly near.

Hereward Brunswick was staying there too with a young female minder, and he joined us for dinner the first night. Linny said afterwards her thigh was black and blue, but I warned her not to sit too near to him because I had got his measure at Mallard Rise.

I'd begged Linny to come to the writers' panel event for support since I was quite nervous about being there with all those terribly serious literary types; but actually it was a *big* mistake, because when someone in the audience asked me whether I aspired to write something a bit *better* than chick lit one day and I replied that I didn't consider myself a chick-lit writer in the *first* place (old broiler, maybe?), and this man persisted...

Well, then Linny stood up, all five foot nine of her bristling with indignation (I keep telling her about that facial hair, she really should have kept those laser appointments), and said I was more *dick lit* than *chick lit* – but then *he* wouldn't know about *that*, would he?

Then she turned scarlet and sat down suddenly and so did the man, and Hereward bobbed up at the back and shouted, 'Hear, hear!'

There was this stunned silence – you could have heard a page turn in the next tent – and the chairman wasn't doing anything except catching flies with his mouth, so I looked around and said brightly, 'Anyone got any more questions?'

The chairman finally pulled himself together. 'Actually, Ms ... er ... Devino, we've run out of time.' Then he thanked the panel, though he gave *me* a strange look and I don't somehow think they will be asking me again, unfortunately, because I enjoyed it in a strange sort of way, and poor Linny has probably been blackballed from anything literary for ever.

But I still had to do my little talk next day, so I suggested tactfully to Linny after the panel thing that perhaps she might like to go to one of the *other* talks rather than mine?

She said she was so sorry, she was absolutely mortified and she didn't know what had come over her, even when I assured her it was worth it to see everyone's faces, but she wanted to turn tail and flee for home.

'No, we're here for the duration, Linny, and we're damned well going to enjoy ourselves!' I informed her, and she was sulking a bit until she spotted an old beekeeper's hat in an antique shop and insisted on wearing it immediately with the veil down, and only took it off for meals.

And actually it worked *terribly* well because everyone thought she was someone famous incognito and so I got fame by proximity; and in that safari suit with the *unfortunate* breast pockets and the billowing waistline that could have hidden six pregnancies, and bearing in mind the scale she's built on, she could have been absolutely *anyone*, male or female, but with a leaning towards the Attenboroughs.

My talk on the sexual imagery of flowers seemed well attended, but mostly by men, oddly enough, and some of the questions *were* a bit offbeat in a scholarly sort of way. Strangely, there seemed to be a clear division between the literary academics who would quite happily argue minor points and references all day in a dry-as-dust finicky manner, and the loose cannons like Hereward Brunswick, who just wanted to dig dirt.

But they *all* seemed to have read the newspaper serialization of Sergei's memoirs and had made their own minds up about me, and why men should think that because I get up to fun and frolics with *one* man, I'm up for it with *any* of them I simply don't understand, especially if they've looked in the mirror within living memory, but so it always is. I had to verbally slap a few of them around the head before I could escape from the tent with my virtue more or less intact.

Oh, and Elvira Pucklington was there, because she introduced herself afterwards and said she was a huge fan, and she knew my aunt, the *other* Tina Devino, who had been a great help in getting her published.

'Oh, yes, she's a batty old tart and I'm afraid we've rather lost touch, but I hear she's living quietly in Shrimphaven running some kind of literary agency, these days,' I said quickly, and just then Hereward bounced up and said he was going to escort me to the refreshment tent for a stiff bracer, which was all right by me as long as *he* wasn't it.

When I staggered out into the sunshine again I found Linny had been searching for me and she said, 'Why do people keep asking me for my autograph?'

'Because you look like someone famous, but they don't know who, so they're hedging their bets. What did you sign as?'

'Sigmunda Rigley, my pen name for M and

B,' she said proudly, so that must have puzzled them.

I went to Hereward's talk, which was a lot of entertainingly salacious froth, really, about his recent book-signing tour and what else he had put – or tried to put – his name on besides books. The audience listened to him with total respect because he was (a) male and (b) writing thrillers, which were mostly read by men, and so obviously several rungs up the literary ladder above my mere romances.

And at the end, when someone asked him where he got his inspiration from, as they always do, he said he got most of the inspiration for the purple passages from beautiful ladies of his acquaintance and then he winked at me and tossed me the pink carnation from his buttonhole.

I can think of several words to describe Hereward, but irrepressible is the only one you could repeat in polite company.

Thirty-One

Picture This

NOVELTINA LITERARY AND CRITICAL AGENCY
Mudlark Cottage, The Harbour, Shrimphaven.

Dear Ms Mendosa,
  Thank you for your new manuscript, Tears of the Mangrove, *a sequel to your first. And thank you also for the bundle of East Caribbean currency. I am sure you are quite right about the exchange rate.*
  I do admire your perseverance in continuing to write in English instead of exploring the Spanish markets for your interesting works, despite your lack of success in placing Voice of the Mangrove *to date. And it is always a bit of a gamble writing a sequel to something that hasn't yet been published.*
  Actually, your grasp of English has improved in this one, making it much easier to read, though I have pointed out in the margins where you have gone somewhat astray with the grammar.
  The major problem I can see is that the plot is

more or less the same as the first: the beautiful, recently widowed, very young Cuban heroine finds that she is not quite so well-provided for by her late husband as she expected and so travels to Grand Cayman in search of husband number two. Like her first, her new husband is old, American, overweight, and very, very rich (she checks that out thoroughly this time, which readers might find just a little cold-blooded). Then he dies in that freak boating accident while they are sailing together in his yacht, leaving her adrift alone in the vast Caribbean sea until she is rescued by attractive tourist-boat-boy Dessie.

Mind you, I'm not saying that this one won't sell, though readers may find it hard to empathize with a heroine who, however young and beautiful, is so clearly on the make.

Anyway, you will find my full critique enclosed, and I will send it addressed to your friend on St Lucia as you requested. I am sorry to hear that the trouble you were having with the authorities on Grand Cayman (although you didn't say exactly what), caused you to have to leave the island so suddenly, and without most of your treasured possessions. But how fortunate that your new boyfriend has his own boat!

Hope everything has been resolved by the time you get this.

With best wishes,
Tina Devino

I have spent many happy hours rearranging and nurturing the plants in Sergei's conservatory while Linny has done much the same for the room she is transforming into a nursery, both sets of activities probably being facets of the same innate urge.

Since he bought the biggest specimen of everything on the list that he could, it won't surprise me if Sergei will be picking his own bananas without leaving the house very soon, not to mention pineapples.

Of course, he would actually have to get up off the wicker daybed to do that, where he lazily reclines like a pasha, sipping tea while watching me and making earthy suggestions, not all to do with the plants.

Sergei's book launch party was like a repeat of our engagement party on a *much* larger scale, and was held in an art gallery, but lots of the guests were invited by the publishers so we didn't know who half of them were.

As I stood next to him, sipping pink champagne while we talked about our respective writings to all kinds of people, it occurred to me that this was *it*: I was now a *success*.

Not only have I just signed a new and lucrative contract with Crimp & Letchworth, I'm also engaged to a gorgeous and very famous man, while still having plenty of time to lust after other men as the fancy and inspiration takes me. Everything's going *so* well...

Then Miracle (whom *I* certainly didn't invite) loomed up with a one-hit-wonder in tow, but don't ask me which one, because they all look the same to me, and congratulated me on the deal and the engagement. Then she said I remembered Tanya, didn't I? And had I heard? Tanya here had sold the film rights to her new book, and she was sure it would be a big commercial success.

Nathan suddenly appeared behind me and said, 'Don't you mean they've taken an *option* on it, Miracle? There's many an option taken up that never gets to be a film, but well done anyway, Tanya.'

And that was quite sharp of him, I think, but I was still staring at Tanya and thinking, wow, a film! Now *there* was a possibility I'd never even thought of before...

As Miracle, smiling stiffly, moved away like a barge attended by a light and giddy skiff, I grasped Nathan by the arm and said urgently, 'Nathan, about film rights—'

I was right about Sergei's book, because it has bounded up the charts like a monkey up a banana tree, and he was asked to write a biography of a ballerina but he said no, he wasn't interested in any other dancer's career, which is honest.

He certainly doesn't need the money either, being cleverer with his investments than people would expect, so his ballet teaching and SergeiYoga classes are because he likes doing them. He just sort of presides over the exercise classes anyway, which are actually taken by relays of out-of-work ballet dancers, though he still spends hours every day exercising, though what he is keeping fit *for* I leave to your imagination, but at least he will be in trim for the new exercise DVD when they start to shoot it.

Ballet in some form is his life, just as writing is mine, *and* the critiquing, which I *could* give up now of course, though I think I would really miss it, and so I'm not going to stop just yet.

And let's be practical here: how many novelists sign a big contract with a major publisher and then that's the last you ever hear of them? They don't earn out their vast advance, the next one's given *no* publicity, and then it's 'goodbye, we'll have to let you go...' I could *still* go up with the rocket and down with the stick, and I could name you a round half-dozen off the top of my head who've done just that.

Nathan says I'm paranoid, I've *made* it, but I tell him, 'Not until one of my novels is a film!'

And *The Orchid Huntress*, which I've now

finished bar a polish, could be the one to break into the wonderful world of moving pictures, preferably before some bright spark decides Sergei's spicy memoirs would make an even better one.

But who on earth could they get to play his part? It's like there can only ever *be* one truly amazingly attractive male ballet star at a time, and he is *it* for his generation, though Grigor is shaping up *very* well for the next.

Linny is busy writing another Mills and Boon while awaiting the advent of her off-spring, but has also suddenly gained a keen interest in genealogy and is tracing her family history, which apparently now numbers an exiled Slavic princeling among her ancestors, though it's the first I've heard of it.

Mind you, she says anything is possible when you have a Lebanese grandmother, which is unanswerable really, but surely records are harder to trace out there?

However, she looked perfectly unself-conscious while telling Tershie all about her findings while I was there one day, so I think I have a deeply suspicious mind to think she might just be hedging her bets.

But our lives have all settled into a per-fectly acceptable new pattern, so I have no intention of stirring anything up, and I don't see why I can't go on like this for ever, only hopefully with more bestsellers and a film or two and a bit of security in the form of a queen's ransom in diamonds.

Thirty-Two

Sour Cream

This morning I was sitting in Sergei's tropical conservatory thinking happy thoughts and sipping tea out of a gilded pink tumbler, while he whipped up blinis and sour cream to go with the inevitable caviar, which I am resigned to now, because I could have fallen for a Scandinavian who are apparently all mad about herring and have it at every meal according to Jackie, who once worked in Sweden for six months. So, thank my lucky stars for that one.

The sun was warm, the birds and Sergei were singing, my rocket was still rising and my bolt-hole by the sea was secure.

Sergei came in carrying a tray and smiling. 'That was Nathan on the phone. Did you not hear me call? The film rights, he thinks the option will be taken up.'

I sat up straight and stared. 'The film rights to *Travels Through a Life*?' I demanded.

313

'No, my darling: to *Dark, Passionate Earth*.' He put the tray down on the low table, sat down next to me and took my hand, the one with the big sparkly ring on it that was casting refracted rainbows all over everything.

'You know, Tsarina,' he said softly, 'the upstairs tenant's lease is about to expire and I am thinking that now we could convert the property back into one big house – big enough for both of us to be together always, but still have our own space – our own apartments, if you wish. So maybe we should turn this engagement into a marriage – have a family, even. What do you think?'

He pressed my hand tenderly to his lips, while I gazed down at his glossy, blue-black hair, totally tongue-tied.

What did I *think*? I thought he'd had a brain transplant, personally, but off the top of my head I simply couldn't think of a polite way of putting it, since clearly a resounding, 'No *way*!' would have been totally inappropriate in the circumstances.

My mind was still discarding phrases of acute disinclination for the idea while he prepared a blini with his long, elegant fingers and delivered it to me with one of his sexy, lightly demented smiles, which have started exerting their old magic on me now that his face is unfreezing.

Then the answer that I hoped would put him off the idea *without* putting off our engagement came to me in a *blinding* flash, as do most of my better inspirations!

I expect *you* got it first? But then, bear in mind that you didn't have Sergei Popov in close proximity, addling your brains.

Yes, it was confession time – truth or dare.

'Sergei, that's a terribly sweet idea, but I'm afraid I have a confession to make. You know I admitted last birthday to being thirty-five—'

'But of course,' he said. 'And the one before. Why not? Do I tell the truth when a lie is kinder to myself?'

'Yes, but Sergei,' I persevered, 'I'm *much, much* older than that, and I'm afraid children are quite out of the question!'

'Ah, do not give up hope, my darling!' he said, embracing me warmly. 'For you are the same age as Linny, I know, you were at school together: that is clearly not too old!'

'But you can't *possibly* want children, Sergei! You've never shown the least interest in them,' I protested.

'I have seen the way you look at Linny, my Tina, and know what is in your heart. And children? Why not? Am I not still virile?'

'Let's not go there,' I said tartly, and he looked slightly puzzled, but while I may have *forgiven*, forgetting is another matter.

'I need the sea – I need to be alone in my cottage sometimes,' I tried to explain, sounding a bit Marlene Dietrich.

'And I too sometimes wish to be alone, to play the sad Russian songs of my youth. That is good, and when we are together, that is *also* good. So we are alike, and it will work, you will see.'

I'd temporarily run out of stalling manoeuvres, and the invidious suggestion regarding procreation – which is something I'd never seriously even *thought* of in connection with myself until Linny suddenly set off on her journey into brink-of-menopause motherhood, leaving me behind – was beginning to have a certain appalling fascination, like an offer to try bungee jumping over the Grand Canyon.

I was simply too punch drunk to react when he sprang up and started phoning my brother Tony and then all his friends to announce our imminent nuptials, and I should think the bread makers and toasters will soon be arriving by every post...

But if anyone can think of a way of freeing me from this strangely fascinating nightmare scenario, please, please do write urgently to me: Tina Devino at Noveltina Literary and Critical Agency, Mudlark Cottage, The Harbour, Shrimphaven.

And I'll send you a personally signed copy

316

of *The Orchid Huntress* upon publication, I promise, together with my undying gratitude.

The diamonds are negotiable.